An unexpected journey.

I tore myself away from the joy of letting the wind blow my ears around and gave Drover a sour look. "Alpine? Alpine refers to a range of mountains called the Alps. The Alps are in a distant state, perhaps Oklahoma or New York City. Why would we be going to such a place?"

"Well, I don't know. I heard Slim say something about Alpine. I just wondered."

"Drover, it's good that you wonder about things every once in a while, and I've tried to encourage you to use your little mind whenever possible, but I can assure you that this is just a routine trip to town. We are not going to Alpine."

"Then how come Slim packed up all his clothes? And his saddle? See, they're sitting on the seat of the pickup."

Huh? To be honest, I had missed that tiny detail.

Slim's Good-bye

HANK
THE COWDOG®

John R. Erickson

Illustrations by Gerald L. Holmes

Puffin Books

PUFFIN BOOKS
Published by the Penguin Group
Penguin Putnam Books for Young Readers,
345 Hudson Street, New York, New York 10014, U.S.A.
Penguin Books Ltd,
27 Wrights Lane, London W8 5TZ, England
Penguin Books Australia Ltd,
Ringwood, Victoria, Australia
Penguin Books Canada Ltd,
10 Alcorn Avenue, Toronto, Ontario, Canada M4V 3B2
Penguin Books (N.Z.) Ltd,
182-190 Wairau Road, Auckland 10, New Zealand

Penguin Books Ltd, Registered Offices:
Harmondsworth, Middlesex, England

Published simultaneously by Viking and Puffin Books, members
of Penguin Putnam Books for Young Readers, 2000

11 13 15 17 19 20 18 16 14 12

LIBRARY OF CONGRESS CATALOGING-IN-PUBLICATION DATA
Erickson, John R., date
Slim's goodbye / by John R. Erickson ; illustrations by Gerald L. Holmes.
p.   cm. — (Hank the cowdog ; 34)
Summary: When the ranch falls on hard times, Slim the cowboy
decides to hit the road in search of a new job and inadvertently
takes Hank and Drover with him.
ISBN: 0-14-130677-7
[1. Dogs Fiction. 2. Cowboys Fiction. 3. Ranch life Fiction. 4. West (U.S.)
Fiction. 5. Humorous stories.] I. Holmes, Gerald L., ill. II. Title. III. Series:
Erickson, John R., date Hank the cowdog ; 34.
PZ7.E72556S1 2000 [Fic]—dc21 99-36113 CIP Rev.

Hank the Cowdog® is a registered trademark of John R. Erickson.

Printed in the United States of America

For my friends at Puffin Books.

CONTENTS

CHAPTER ONE

Scrap Time
on the Ranch

It's me again, Hank the Cowdog. Who would have ever thought that Slim would quit his job on the ranch and leave? Not me.

Pretty sad, huh? I mean, Slim and I were special pals. We'd spent years working together on the ranch. I never would have dreamed . . .

But I'm getting ahead of myself. Where were we? Oh yes, the beginning of the day. Morning. It appeared to be a normal morning in December—cloudy, cold, gray, wind blowing out of the north. Drover and I were sleeping late that morning, when all at once my ears shot up and I was awakened by the sound of a door slamming up at the house.

1

Do you realize what this meant? Maybe not, if you're not a dog.

Scrap Time!

If you're a dog, very few moments in the history of this world have more meaning or importance than Scrap Time. It gives purpose and direction to our lives, fills them with meaning and hope. And so it was that, upon hearing the slamming of the screen door, I came roaring out of deep sleep, leaped out of my gunnysack bed, cranked open the outer doors of my eyes, and shouted the news to Drover.

"Hurry, Drover, it's tinted feathers, and they all weigh a ton!"

By that time he had joined me in an upright position. "Who? What? How many?"

"I don't know, Drover, I didn't have time to count them, but two thousand feathers weigh a ton." We stared at each other. "What did I just say?"

"I don't know. Something about . . . feathers. I think that's what you said."

"I did not say anything about feathers."

"Oh, okay. Maybe it was me."

"Of course it was you, and I must warn you not to talk about feathers."

He yawned. "How come?"

"Don't yawn while I'm speaking to you."

"Sorry. I just woke up."

"It gives the impression that you're bored."

"Not me. I just woke up."

"You already said that."

"Oh. Sorry. I'm liable to say anything. I just woke up."

I glared at the runt. "That makes three times you've said that."

"I'll be derned. I must have been asleep."

"Of course you were. If you just woke up, it follows from simple logic that . . . something woke us up, Drover, something very important. What was it?"

"Well, I heard a bunch of feathers."

"Feathers? How can you hear feathers?"

"Well . . . I don't know. I can't hear 'em now."

"There were no feathers, Drover, except the ones where your brains ought to be."

"Maybe that was it, 'cause I'm almost sure I heard 'em."

"You did *not* hear them."

"That's what I meant. I didn't hear any feathers, and maybe that's what woke us up."

"Hmmm. Could be, although . . . wait, I've got it now. I had just heard the screen door slam up at the house. Do you realize what this means?"

"Well, let's see. Someone came out of the house?"

"Right. Keep going."

"Someone came out of the house through the door?"

"Good. Excellent. Keep going. Put your clues together. What do they add up to?"

"Let's see here. Five?"

"No."

"Ten?"

"We're not looking for a number."

"Oh. I thought you wanted me to add up all my clues."

"No, I wanted you to follow your clues and tell me why someone came out of the house."

"Okay, I'll get it this time." He rolled his eyes and twisted his mouth around. I could see that the effort of concentrating was taking its toll on him. "Twelve?"

The air hissed out of my body. I walked a few steps away and tried to clear my head. I've always tried to help Drover, to bring him along and teach him the Security Business, but sometimes I'm not sure he can be helped. I returned to the spot where he was sitting. He gave me his usual silly grin and began wig-wagging that stump tail of his.

"Drover, let's go back to the beginning. Review your list of clues. Don't count them. *Review* them, and follow them to a logical conclusion."

"Well, let's see here. Clues. Door. House." All at once his eyes popped open. "Oh my gosh, Hank, do you reckon it's Scrap Time?"

"Excellent! Very good, Drover. At last you have . . ." He vanished. One minute he was there, and the next he was gone. I made a dash up the hill and caught up with him. "Drover, wait, we're not finished with the lesson. Stop, halt!"

He stopped. "Yeah, but it's Scrap Time."

"I know that, and congratulations on figuring it out. But you forgot to make the last step in the procedure."

"I did?"

"Yes, you did. Don't you remember? After putting all the clues together and coming up with the right answer, you have to return to the gas tanks and touch base."

"I do? How come?"

"Because that's the way it's done. You have to touch base to restart the system."

"I'll be derned. I didn't think of that."

I gave him a fatherly pat on the shoulder. "That's why I'm here, son, to remind you of things and to help you along. Now go tag up."

"Okay, and what'll you do?"

"I'll, uh, wait here and cheer you on."

5

"Okay, here I go!"

He went zooming down to the gas tanks. I gave him one loud cheer and then, heh heh, hurried up to the yard gate to check out the scrap business. It proved to be pretty interesting.

I was pleased and excited to see Little Alfred standing on the back porch. I was even pleaseder when I saw the plate in his hand.

I made my way to the yard gate, sat down, and shifted into a routine we call Loyal Friend Waiting Patiently for Scraps. I knew it would work on the boy. We were the best of pals, don't you know, and he had always shown excellent judgment when it came to giving the scraps to me instead of to his momma's precious kitty. Pete, that is.

Pete didn't happen to be in sight at that moment, but I knew it was only a matter of time until he showed up. He always showed up when he wasn't wanted. Throw a picnic and the flies will come out of nowhere. Show up on the back porch with breakfast scraps and Mister Kitty Moocher will come slinking out of the iris patch.

But if we hurried this deal along, heh heh, maybe there wouldn't be anything left for him, heh heh, or for Drover. And so I turned up the Urgency Knob and caught the boy's attention. He saw me and waved.

6

"Hi, Hankie. Want some scwaps?"

Oh yes, please! I hadn't eaten in months . . . okay, hours . . . I hadn't eaten in hours, had shrunk down to skin and bones, and was in desperate need of food. Anything, just any little morsel he could spare, such as . . . well, juicy fatty ends of bacon, a piece of fried egg white, a scrap of toast sopped in egg yolk . . . just any little scrap he happened to have on the plate.

He came toward me and opened the gate. "Come on in the yard, Hankie, and we'll pway Catch the Scwap."

Well, I . . . maybe that wasn't such a great idea. I mean, I loved playing Catch the Scrap with the boy. We'd played it many times and I had proved myself to be one of the best scrap catchers in all of Texas, but Sally May, his mommy, had rules against dogs in the yard. It was a silly rule—also terribly unfair to us dogs—but I had no wish to get involved, so to speak, with Sally May first thing in the morning. Or any other time.

Alfred grinned, tossed a glance over his shoulder, and whispered, "Mom's inside feeding my sister. She'll never know you came into the yard."

Ha! Was he kidding? Sally May knew *everything*. She had radar. She had eyes in the back of her head. She had STP . . . PDQ . . . whatever it is when you know things and see things that others don't know or see.

No, as much as I would have enjoyed playing Catch the Scrap in the yard . . .

He shouldn't have held that piece of bacon in front of my nose. I have very few weaknesses, very few clinks in my armor, but bacon held up in front of my nose is one of them. It seems to melt my iron discipline and turns me into a . . . something. A robot who can think of nothing but yummy bacon, I suppose.

Alfred knew that, but he did it anyway. He held that bacon in front of my nose and lured me through the open gate and across the line into Sally May's Forbidden Yard. I couldn't help myself. The bacon vapors filled my nostrils and took control of my mind, and I had no choice but to follow that bacon wherever it led.

He had duped me, tricked me, used my weakness against me, forced me to break the First Rule of Ranch Law, and when he pitched the bacon into the air, I snagged that rascal and gulped it down. No dog in history had ever enjoyed breaking the law more than I, and as far as I was concerned, we could play Catch the Scrap for the rest of the . . .

HUH?

I heard a creak as the back door opened. My

ears flew up. I froze and found myself staring into Alfred's eyes, which had grown big and round. Then I heard him utter some shocking words: "Oops. It's my mom."

I knew it. I'd tried to tell him. She always showed up at the very worst times. She had radar for naughty thoughts. A dog wasn't safe on that ranch until she went to town, and even then a guy couldn't get over the feeling that she was still there, watching and listening and lurking around the next corner.

In a flash, I transformed myself into Rocket Dog and flew back across the line, struck a calm, relaxed pose on the Dog Side of the fence, and, uh, worked my face around so that it showed . . . well, mild surprise on seeing her come out of the house, delight that she had decided to, uh, join us, and above all, perfect innocence.

I gave her my most sincere cowdog smile, as if to say, "Oh my goodness, it's Sally May, my very favorite ranch wife! What a pleasure to see you this morning. Alfred and I were just . . . well, doing nothing really, just listening to the chirping of the birds and enjoying the, uh, beauty of the morning . . . so to speak. Nothing else. Really. No kidding."

She saw us at once. Her eyes speared me. She

came down the sidewalk toward us. Alfred had begun to whistle and was looking up at the sky. I studied her face to see if our program was selling. I couldn't tell.

CHAPTER TWO

I Play Mind Games
with the Cat

Sally May stopped and loomed over us like a thunderhead cloud. Her gaze went from me to Alfred and back to me. When it was on me, I could feel the heat of it. It was hard for me to keep up my casual smile, but somehow I managed to do it.

"Well. What have we here?"

"Oh, hi, Mom. We were just . . . goofin' awound."

"Goofing around. Did you happen to notice that the gate is open?"

Alfred's eyes turned to the open gate. "Gosh. The wind must have bwone it open."

Her left eyebrow rose. "The wind did not blow it open. You opened it and you were trying to feed Hank in my yard, weren't you?"

The boy's head sank into his shoulders. "Well, he was hungwy."

"Of course he was hungry. He's always hungry, but you can't feed him in my yard." Her eyes swung around to me. "No dogs in the yard. Period. Ever. Is that clear, Hank?"

I felt myself melting under the beam of her eyes. Yes ma'am.

She turned back to the boy. "Is that clear, Alfred Leroy?"

"Yes ma'am. But I think it was the wind."

A thin smile slid across her mouth. "Don't try to tell whoppers to your mother. I know boys and I know dogs. What one of you doesn't think up, the other one will. Oh, and save some of the scraps for the other animals. It isn't fair for Hank to get them all."

And with that, she cupped her hands around her mouth and called Drover and her precious kitty. In a flash, Drover was there, huffing and puffing.

"Hi, Hank. I touched base and made it in time for scraps. Are you proud of me?"

I gave him a glare. "You bet. I was worried sick you might not make it."

"Gosh, thanks. And you waited on the scraps until I got here, huh?"

"Oh yes. It wouldn't have been fair if I'd gotten

all the . . . Drover, did you touch base once or twice?"

"Well, let's see. Once. That's what you said."

"Darn. I guess I forgot to tell you."

His grin vanished. "Tell me what?"

"Well, you're supposed to touch base twice. I thought you knew that. I mean, I thought everybody knew that. It's common knowledge."

"It is?"

"Sure. If you touch base only once . . . well, I'm sure you can guess what might happen."

"Is it bad?"

"Oh yes, very bad. It's so bad, I can't even say it out loud."

He was looking worried by this time. "Gosh. Can you whisper it?"

"Better not. Just try to imagine the worst thing that might happen."

He thought about it for a minute. "Not *that*."

"Yes, Drover. *That*."

"That would be awful."

"See? Didn't I tell you? It just doesn't pay to cut corners."

"Yeah, and maybe I'd better run back down there and touch base again."

I gave him a wink and a nod. "Great idea, Drover. And what makes it even greater is that you came up with it on your own."

"Yeah, I feel so proud. Maybe I'm smarter than I thought."

"Oh? How smart did you think you were?"

"Not very."

"I think you're on the right trail, son."

"Thanks, Hank. Here I go!"

And with that, he went zooming back down to the gas tanks, which left me and Little Alfred with all the, heh heh, scraps. I turned to him and switched into a little routine we call I'll Die If I Don't Get Those Scraps. It seemed to be working. He plucked a juicy fatty end of bacon off the plate and was about to toss it into the air when . . . oops. She was still there.

Madame Radar.

Alfred's mother.

Sally May. "Alfred! Wait for the cat. Here kitty kitty kitty. Come on, Petey, come for scraps."

We waited. I hate waiting, and the kind of hating I wait the most is waiting for a cat. What a waste of time. What a waste of good scraps. I really dislike cats a lot.

Well, at last Pete showed himself. Do you think he came running? Oh no. If he hadn't been called, he would have come out of the bushes like a little rocket, and he'd have been crawling all over Alfred to mooch some scraps. But since he'd been called, since we had all been forced to wait for His Worthless Highness, he came at a slow walk.

He was purring, of course, and wearing that grin that drives me nuts. He stepped out of the iris patch and rubbed his way down the side of the house until he reached the porch. There, he rubbed against the northwest corner of the porch and waltzed down the sidewalk until he came to Sally May. He made three circles around her, rubbing on her legs as though he loved her so much he just couldn't contain himself.

The little fraud. He knew we couldn't eat until he got there. He knew I was dying of bacon lust. He knew he had a captive audience and that he had become the center of attention, so naturally he was playing it for all it was worth, enjoying every second of the torment he was causing.

That's a cat for you, a totally selfish egomechanic. They love to torment others, you know, and to mooch scraps. And Pete was the most shameless scrap-moocher I'd ever known.

Well, as he was circling Sally May's ankles, he was also tossing winks and grins in my direction. Oh yes, I saw the whole shabby deal, and I knew exactly what the little sneak was up to. He wanted to get me stirred up, see, right there in front of Sally May.

Ha! Little did he know that I had already plotted out my response. I had a plan for Pete. I was ready for him this time.

See, a lot of dogs—and we're talking here about your lower grades of ranch dogs, the kind that never rise through the ranks to become Heads of Ranch Security—a lot of your ordinary ranch mutts would have fallen for Pete's sneakiness like a hill of beans.

The thing you have to remember about cats, and Pete in particular, is that they're not very smart, but they're not very smart in a cunning sort of way. There's a certain cleverness about them, and a guy needs to approach them with caution. You have to guard yourself against overconfidence, is the main thing.

Just because they're dumb doesn't mean they can't get you into trouble.

Well, I had gone to school on cats. I had spent hours and days and years studying their tactics, analyzing their schemes and tricks, and preparing defenses against them. You've heard of chess? Well, we dogs are chess players. It requires patience and huge reserves of brain power, and when we go one-on-one against a cat in the Chess Game of Life, the poor cat doesn't have a chance.

Heh heh. I was ready for the little sneak. Yes sir, I could read his thoughts like a book.

On the third or fourth trip around Sally May's ankles, he turned his grinning face in my direction and said, "Hi, Hankie. Are you waiting for someone?"

I must admit that his whiny voice caught me slightly off guard. My ears leaped to Attack Position and a growl began to rumble in my throat. But don't worry. I caught it just in the nickering of time and got everything shut down before any serious damage was done. I don't think Sally May heard or saw any of it, is how quickly I responded to the crisis.

Hencely, instead of growling and so forth, I gave him a pleasant smile. "Why Pete, how nice to see

you this morning. And yes, we're waiting for you to come and share the scraps."

"What a sweet doggie! I never knew you believed in sharing."

"Oh yes, Pete. I enjoy sharing. I love sharing. Sharing is what this old life is all about."

"But I know how you hate to . . . wait." He grinned and wiggled his stupid . . . wiggled his eyebrows, I should say, which didn't bother me at all. "Waiting has always been hard for you, hasn't it Hankie?"

"Oh no, not really. I have my thoughts to keep me occupied."

"That fills the first two seconds. Then what?"

I gave him a wise chuckle. "Pete, you're losing your touch. I know what you're trying to do, and it just won't work. Sorry."

At that moment, Sally May interrupted us. "All right, Alfred, now you can give out the scraps, and start with Pete."

I beamed her a dark glare. What was the deal? Who'd gotten there first, who'd been waiting patiently for . . . but I didn't care who got first scraps. I could be a gentleman about it—and hope that Pete choked on his scraps.

Alfred tweezed a juicy end of bacon between his thumb and . . . why had he picked the biggest, fattiest piece? That didn't seem right or fair. Who'd been . . . but I didn't care.

(See, not caring was an important part of my plan. Maybe you'd already picked that up.)

Anyway, Alfred held the bacon in front of Pete's nose. He sniffed at it, stared at it with those big yellowish eyes of his, and finally raised a paw and snagged it with his claws. He laid it on the ground, sniffed it some more, licked it, and then looked up at Alfred.

And then he said—you won't believe this—he said, "Is this the best piece, or do you have a better one?"

My eyes almost bugged out of my head when I heard that. There I was, dying of bacon hunger, roasting on the fires of starvation, waiting in line for him to . . . I caught myself just in time and noticed that Kitty was watching me.

I beamed up a smile. "Take your time, Pete. Shop around. We want you to have the very best. And if that piece doesn't suit you, here, let me . . ."

"Hank!"

Oops. That was Sally May and, okay, maybe I'd jumped the gun just a tad. Timing is very important in these deals, and just to prove that I was being sincere, I gave Sally May a look that said, "Just trying to help. No kidding."

It worked. I know it worked because she said, "That's better. Nice dog."

Heh heh. Little did she know what evil thoughts lurked . . . but then, she wasn't supposed to know. I had her fooled, that was the important thing.

I sat down again and watched Kitty-Kitty play with his bacon. Can you believe that? He had this gorgeous, great-smelling piece of bacon fat right there in front of his stupid . . . right in front of his nose, and *he played with it*! He patted it. He speared it on his claws, held it up, stared at it, sniffed it, licked it, pitched it up, pushed it around, and oh yes, every so often he would cut his eyes in my direction to check my reaction.

Luckily, he couldn't see my reaction. It was all happening inside, and there was quite a lot of it. My eyes were bulging, my heart was racing, my breaths were coming in rapid bursts, my mouth was watering, and above it all, I kept hearing this voice that said, "Open outer doors, flood tubes one and three, and plot a solution."

Do you know what that means? It means that one part of my inner bean was urging me to attack, pounce on the little sneak, and give him the thrashing he so richly deserved. But I caught myself just in time and kept it all inside.

Or I tried. This was about to drive me nuts. I

turned pleading eyes toward my pal, eyes that said, "Alfred, this is cruel and unfair. Do something."

You know what? He did. He checked out his mom, saw that she was looking away, and in a flash he snatched the bacon away from Mister Hateful, flipped it into the air, and . . . heh heh . . . I took care of the rest.

Old Pete was so shocked, he didn't know what to say. But then he started getting mad.

"You stole my bacon, Hankie."

That was right. And what did he plan to do about it?

CHAPTER THREE

Dark Clouds Gather

You're probably thinking that I allowed myself to get drawn into a fight with Pete, and that I got into big trouble with Sally May.

Nope. Iron Discipline prevailed, kept me safe and out of trouble. Pretty impressive, huh?

Okay, maybe I did feel myself being pulled into a major confrontation with Mister Greedy Scrap Stealer, and maybe it did appear that I might lose control of the situation. I mean, what dog could just sit there and watch Pete hog all the scraps?

There we were, the cat and I, standing nose-to-nose. He arched his back and began to yowl, and you know what that yowling does to me. It brings all my savage instincts rushing to the surface. I lifted my lips and exposed two rows of deadly,

23

enormous teeth, and a growl began to rumble in the depths of my throat.

Yes, it appeared that we were rushing toward a major episode, and suddenly I was helpless to pull myself back from the brink of the edge. I glared into the face of the yowling cat and began plotting all the targeting data that would . . .

You know what saved me? Slim. Just then, he drove up in his pickup, honked his horn, and yelled, "Come on, dogs, let's go feed those cattle!" He must have noticed that I was . . . well, all bristled up and ready to launch a strike against the cat. He yelled, "Hank, leave the cat alone and come on. We're burning daylight."

I took a step backward and began the Disengagement Procedure. I switched over to Friendly Tail, lowered the strip of hair down the middle of my back, and closed the outer doors of my Tooth Torpedoes.

"Excuse me, Kitty, but I've just been called out on an important mission. Your daily thrashing will have to wait. I have more important things to do."

He gave me a sour smile. "Well, just darn the luck. I had you going there for a minute."

"Ha! You had nothing, Kitty. Everything was going according to my plan."

24

"Now I'll have to eat the rest of the scraps myself. Darn."

Slim honked his horn again. I began backing away. "Yes, and I hope you choke on them. I wish you nothing but fleas and bedsores and ringworms, Pete. We'll settle this score another time."

And with that, I whirled around and marched away, leaving the cat standing in the rubble of his own shambles. Also playing with MY bacon scraps, the little pest, but . . . oh well.

The important thing is that Slim needed help feeding the east side of the ranch, and you'll notice that he invited me, not the cat, to help him. And I did. I made a huge contribution to the feeding process, and by noon we had fed four pastures.

We returned to ranch headquarters around twelve. I had seen no sign or symptom that Slim was brooding about anything. He seemed his usual carefree self. But when we pulled around to the back of the house and walked up to the gate, Loper was standing there. There was a furrow in his brow. His eyes were tight and pinched, and he was staring off into the distance.

Slim walked over toward Loper and immediately leaned against the gatepost. "What's wrong with you?"

"Plenty. I've got to go into town and renew my loan at the bank."

"Uh-oh. I heard on the radio that the cattle market fell out of bed again."

"No, it didn't fall out of bed. It fell off the roof and landed in the commode. It couldn't have come at a worse time. We're out of grass and I've got to buy some hay."

Slim scratched his ear. "That puts bankers in a bad humor."

Loper nodded. "He wants to look at our numbers, numbers on everything: cows, calves, yearlings; the cost of feed, labor, fuel, pickups; every stinking detail. Sally May's been working on it all morning."

"Well, I thought we were doing pretty well. I mean, we ain't exactly been goofing off out here. At the end of the day, I feel like I've worked pretty hard."

Loper shook his head. "That's not it. We work hard enough, all of us. Heck, if hard work was the answer, we'd be loaning money to the banker. But when you don't have any control over the price of your product . . . and when you have to operate on borrowed money . . ."

His voice trailed off into silence.

Slim shifted his weight to the other leg. "Are we in trouble?"

"I don't know. We might be. It all depends on how that banker's feeling at three o'clock this afternoon. A guy never knows."

"Well, I sure don't want to be a burden to y'all. If my paycheck's a problem . . ."

Loper shook his head. "Don't worry about it. We'll take things one day at a time. That's all we can do. How about some lunch?"

"Oh, all at once I ain't feeling so hungry. I might just drift down to my place and grab a little nap."

Loper studied him for a moment. "Now Slim, you're not going to brood about this, are you?"

"Nope."

"Good. It won't help one bit."

"I ain't going to brood about it. I promise." And then he did something odd. He shook hands with Loper and smiled. "I'll see you around, pardner. Good luck at the bank."

And with that, they parted company. At the time, I had no idea . . .

Well, Slim headed for his pickup in that slow walk of his, and naturally I went with him. I mean, he'd mentioned something about a nap, right? And Slim had been known to let dogs into his house, right? Hey, I'd spent the morning working and slaving on the ranch, and the thought of grabbing a few Zs beside the wood-burning stove sounded pretty good to me.

Well, guess who joined us near the gas tanks. Mister Sleep Till Noon. Mister Never Sweat. Drover. He heard us coming and came bouncing over to join us.

"Hi, Hank. Gosh, you're up early this morning."

I gave him a withering glare. "Morning? Ha. Some of us have already put in a day's work."

"Yeah, I hated to miss it, but after I touched base the second time, this old leg was tearing me up. I figured I needed to give it a little rest."

"I see. Well, how's your 'old leg' now? I noticed that you were bouncing around like a little kangaroo."

"Yeah, sleep does wonders. It's almost as good as new."

"Great. Glad to hear it. Oh, and I hope you don't feel guilty about leaving me with the total responsibility of running the ranch."

"Well, it bothers me sometimes, but I know you can handle it. Where we going?"

"I don't know where you're going. I'm going down to Slim's place."

"Oh good, I think I'll tag along. I'm all rested now."

"We're going to take a nap, Slim and I."

"Oh good, me too. I'm just about worn out."

I shot him a sideways glare and . . . oh well. There's no future in trying to talk sense to a dunce.

We loaded up in the cab of the pickup. Slim got in behind us and we headed down the creek to his shack. When we reached the county road, Slim started talking to us.

"You know, boys, for the longest time I've had it in my head to go to Alpine, down in the Davis Mountains, but I never quite made it. Pickup went bust and we got busy with the cattle work . . . one thing and another. I always aimed to get there in the springtime when the snow melted off, but I just never got around to it."

I had a hard time figuring out what he was talking about, but that wasn't exactly the biggest shock of the year. I mean, Slim was the kind of guy who thought out loud, and sometimes what he said . . . well, I hate to put it this way, but sometimes what he said didn't make a whole lot of sense.

Part of my job as Head of Ranch Security is learning how to respond to the humans around here—when to pay attention and when to . . . well, not pay such close attention. What I've learned over the years is that when they're not yelling, most of what they're saying can be ignored. Slim wasn't yelling, so I gave no more thought to his rambling about . . . where was it this time? Alpine?

See, I'd heard him ramble about Alpine before, how he'd always dreamed of riding his horse through the mountains and working on a ranch so big they'd have to bring sunlight in on pack horses. Then he'd laugh at himself and say, "Now, ain't that just like a cowboy? Always dreaming about a place that's bigger and wilder?"

And as far as I knew, he'd never been to Alpine. He'd just talked about it. And I was pretty sure, knowing Slim as I did, that he would never get around to doing it. Too much trouble.

When we reached Slim's shack, we dogs raced to the front door. We always had this little scuffle, don't you know, to see which one of us would get into the house first. It had to do with which one of us would get the choicest spot in front of the stove and the softest piece of carpet. In other words, this was not small bananas . . . potatoes . . . whatever. It was no small matter, and in fact, it was pretty derned important.

But Slim was taking his sweet time. He didn't go straight to the door, but stopped and looked at the shack. "It's been a pretty good place."

Fine, but it was cold outside. Could we hurry this along? Finally he opened the door, and you'll be proud to know that I beat Drover to the stove and nailed down the very best spot. I circled the spot three times, just as we dogs are supposed to do, and flopped down. It was wonderful.

I wasted no time pushing my rowboat of sleep out into the vast sea of . . . something. Dreams, I suppose. I launched myself into the warm embrace of sleep and dreams, and the next thing I knew . . .

Hmmm, that was odd. Something landed on my left ear. I jerked myself out of the warm embrace of so-forth, lifted my head, and cut my eyes from side to . . . What? Another something landed on the top of my head.

What was going on here? I ran a quick Data

Check on the various parts of my enormous body. My ears were at the Full Alert position. I had a sneaking suspicion that we had a flea running loose, and if that was the case, I had every intention of . . .

What? A third something smacked me, this time right between my eyes. It was wet. Was the roof leaking? Okay, that did it. I was wide awake now and ready to do some serious . . .

I looked up. Huh?

You'll never guess what had caused those mysterious drips.

CHAPTER FOUR

On the Road Again

Slim was standing over me. He was holding a cup in his right hand.

You won't believe this. I could hardly believe it myself, and I'd had years of experience with Slim's warped, weird sense of . . .

He was dripping water on my head! Can you believe that? I couldn't. I mean, what kind of person dribbles water on the head of a sleeping dog? What kind of twisted mind . . .

Fine, I could take a hint. If he was so bored that he couldn't think of anything better to do with his time . . . I moved my freight to another part of the house, is what I did, and then went straight into a Glaring Pattern that we call "I Can't Believe You Just Did That."

He gave me a scowl. "Sleepytime's over, pooch. It's time to hit the road."

Fine, but did he have to . . . *drip on me*? I mean, there are ways of waking up a dog without tormenting him. And why didn't he drip on Drover? Oh well.

He opened the door and hooked his thumb toward the outside, and we dogs made our exit. Slim lingered a moment and ran his gaze over the living room, then came out, closed the door, and walked to his pickup. Drover and I were already there, waiting beside the door and ready to launch ourselves up onto the seat of his . . .

It seemed odd that Slim had decided to use his personal pickup instead of the one we always used on the ranch. I couldn't remember him ever using it except when he went to town on personal business. Was that his plan? Maybe so, and that was fine with me, as long as he took me with him. I had already forgiven him for the dribbling incident and I was ready for a little excitement.

So there we were, Drover and I, ready to leap into the cab. But instead of opening the door, Slim stood there for a long moment, looking down at us. "Y'all can't go this time. You'd better stay here and take care of the ranch."

Then he knelt down and kind of gathered us

into his arms and gave us a hug. Now that was really strange. Slim hugging us? After he'd just amused himself by bombarding my head and ears with drips?

Oh well. We'll take hugs anytime they come, and, heh heh, I managed to nail him a good one on the cheek with a wet tongue. Paybacks.

Then he stood up, glanced around the place one last time, and said, "Well, see you around, boys."

And he climbed into his old rattletrap pickup, cranked up the engine, and drove away.

As the pickup pulled away from the old cowcamp shack, I shot a glance at my assistant. "Drover, I have a sneaking suspicion that he's going to town without us."

"Yeah, 'cause there he goes and here we sit."

"Exactly. And when was the last time we saw the bright lights of town?"

"Well, let's see here. I can't remember, it's been so long."

"Exactly my point. Now, we have a choice here. We can stay out here on the ranch and spend the rest of the day barking at sparrows, or we can hitch a ride into town."

"Yeah, but he told us to stay here."

"I'm aware of that, Drover, but sometimes we dogs have to . . . how can I say this?"

"I don't know, but if we're going to hitch a ride into town, we'd better hurry. Once he gets past that first cattle guard, we won't be able to catch him."

We exchanged secret grins. "Good point, son. I couldn't have put it better myself. Let's move out!"

We raced after the pickup, and sure enough, Slim slowed down for the first cattle guard. You know why? That pickup of his was so old and beat up, it might have fallen apart if he'd hit the cattle guard too fast.

Yes, he slowed down for the cattle guard, and by the time he got there he was thinking about keeping his pickup in one piece. And the last thing on his mind was that we dogs might have decided that we needed a trip to town just as much as Slim did. Heh heh.

He never suspected a thing. We flew into the bed of the pickup. Well, I flew. It took Drover several shots, and he had to grunt and scramble, but we got 'er done. It was a pretty impressive piece of work.

Jumping into the back of a moving pickup isn't all that hard, if you've practiced it a few times and know how to do it. See, we had to come from the side—and not just any side. It had to be the right side, and you probably wonder why.

Simple. Slim had a big mirror on the left side of the pickup, and he just might have seen us if we'd come in from the left. That was pretty crafty of us, huh? You bet it was. Oh, and don't forget that if we had messed up the leaping process, we could have fallen to the ground and gotten ourselves smashed by the tires. We didn't, and for very good reason. I was an expert at Pickup Loaderation and had had had . . . had had had . . .

I HAD HAD valuable experience in Smash Avoidance Techniques, there we go, which came in very handy.

Had had. Two hads, not three. I've never found an occasion when three hads were necessary.

Where were we? Oh yes, we pulled off the Pickup Loaderation deal and made it look like a piece of cheese.

Pie.

Cake.

We made it look easy, is the point, and once we'd both made it into the bed of the pickup, we slithered ourselves to the front and scrunched down behind the cab. With a little luck, old Slim would never know that he was now transporting dogs until we were already in town.

He would be mad, of course, but what the heck? Show me a dog who never does anything naughty and I'll show you a dog who never sees the bright lights of town.

Drover and I exchanged winks and grins and settled down for a nice windblown trip into town. I kind of enjoy those trips in the back of the pickup, when the wind causes the tips of my ears to flap around. It's restful.

So there we were, all set for a . . . huh? That was strange. When we came to Wolf Creek Road, Slim turned left instead of right. A right turn would have taken us toward Twitchell, the town where we usually went, whereas a turn to the left would take us . . . well, I wasn't sure where it went. I had gone that direction a couple of times, and we had always been going to Miss Viola's house.

Is that where we were going, to Miss Viola's?

I shot a glance at Drover. "Hmm. I wonder what this means."

He grinned. "Well, it means we're going to get in trouble with Slim, but you know what? I think it's kind of exciting. I never get into trouble."

"You missed the point, Drover. The point is that we just turned left."

"Right."

"No, left."

"Right. We turned left."

"That's what I said."

"Yeah, and I agreed, so I guess we've got it figured out."

"Hmm, yes. But I wonder why we turned left."

"Well . . .'cause Slim did, and he's driving."

I glared at the runt. "You needn't dwell on the obvious, Drover. I know that Slim's driving, but the point is . . . skip it. I'm sorry I brought it up."

There was a long moment of silence. Then Drover said, "I'll be derned. I wonder why we're going this way instead of the other way."

"Because this is the way Slim turned, and he's driving."

"Oh. Well, that makes sense."

When we came to Miss Viola's place, we slowed down, and for a second there I thought Slim was going to turn in at the driveway. But he didn't. He took a long look up at the house, then sped up and kept going.

"Drover, there's something fishy going on here."

"Yeah, and I love fish, everything but the bones and scales. I ate a scale once and got choked."

"Scales are used for weighing the fish. You should never eat the scales. Did you actually chew it up and swallow it?"

"Oh yeah, but then it got hung up in my throat."

"I'm not surprised. Those things are big."

"Yeah, but catfish don't have any scales."

"Well, in a sense you're right, Drover, but in another sense you're wrong. You see, technically speaking, the scales belong to the people who catch the fish, not to the fish themselves. Hencely, you're correct in saying that catfish don't have scales, but neither do . . . name another kind of fish."

"Well, let's see. There's big fish. And little fish."

"Exactly, and because of the vast difference in size between your big fish and your little fish . . . I seem to have lost the thread of this conversation."

"Needles?"

"Ah, yes. For every needle in this life, there is a thimble waiting to push it through the fabric of society." I noticed that his eyes were crossed. "Why are you crossing your eyes at me?"

"I don't know. I guess I'm confused. I don't know what we're talking about."

"Well, neither do I, so why do we go on talking? Could we just drop it?"

"Fine with me. You're the one who started it."

"I was not. I would never start a conversation with you. A dog would have to be insane to start a conversation with you, and if he wasn't insane to start with, he would be after five minutes."

"I'm sorry. I try to be a good dog."

"You can't help it, Drover. You're just . . . forget it, and don't ever speak to me again."

I enjoyed five entire minutes of silence and peace. Then Drover broke the silence. "You know, it's kind of fishy that we're going east on this road. I guess we're not going to Twitchell."

I stared into the huge vacuum of his eyes and wondered how I could find words to express . . . I decided to say nothing.

The minutes passed and we kept driving. When we came to a blacktop highway, Slim turned right. We were heading south. Some tiny particle of Drover's mind seemed to notice this, and he felt the need to comment on it.

"I'll be derned. We're heading south. You don't reckon we're going to Alpine, do you?"

I tore myself away from the joy of letting the wind blow my ears around and gave him a sour look. "Alpine? Alpine refers to a range of mountains called the Alps. The Alps are in a distant state, perhaps Oklahoma or New York City. Why would we be going to such a place?"

"Well, I don't know. I heard Slim say something about Alpine. I just wondered."

"Drover, it's good that you wonder about things every once in a while, and I've tried to encourage you to use your little mind whenever possible, but I can assure you that this is just a routine trip to town. We are not going to Alpine."

"Then how come Slim packed up all his clothes? And his saddle? See, they're sitting on the seat of the pickup."

Huh? To be honest, I had missed that tiny detail.

CHAPTER FIVE

Our Search for the Elusive Penguins

I pushed myself up on all-fours and peeked through the back window, expecting to find . . . hmm, there sat three grocery sacks stuffed with clothes. Also a saddle, two pairs of boots, and a sack filled with books and magazines.

I turned back to Drover. "He must have packed that stuff while we were sleeping, Drover, so we're not able to use it as evidence in this case."

"Yeah, but it's there. You just saw it."

"We didn't actually see him packing the stuff. Therefore, we can't leap to the conclusion that he packed it himself. It might have been packed by . . . I don't know, somebody else. It might have

43

packed itself. This is a very strange world, Drover, and I must remind you that there are many things that we just don't understand."

"Yeah, but he's got all his clothes. And his saddle. That's everything he owns, and I'm starting to get worried. I don't want to go to Alpine!"

"Will you dry up and quit moaning? Who or whom are you going to trust—me or a bunch of illegal evidence?"

"Well . . ."

"Good choice. Now don't you feel better already?"

"Well . . ."

"Great. That settles it. Trust me, Drover, and you won't have to burden your little mind with a bunch of fauna and flora."

"What's fauna and flora?"

"I'm sorry, we're out of time for questions. Lie down and relax. We are NOT going to Alpine."

And with that, we laid down our heads and took a wonderful nap, knowing in our deepest hearts that Slim would never quit the ranch and haul his dogs to some distant corner of the globe.

I don't know where Drover comes up with this stuff. Alpine? How ridiculous.

I awoke when I felt the pickup slowing down. I raised my head and saw . . . hmm, we seemed to be approaching a long bridge. The sign on the bridge said . . . "Canadian River."

Drover saw it too. "Oh my gosh, we're in Canada! I knew it, I want to go home, and this old leg is killing me!"

I told him to hush. How could I think with him squeaking and moaning? Then I jumped into the task of sifting clues and gathering information. Suddenly I found it hard to deny that we were at that very moment crossing into some distant foreign land. I mean, the sign did say Canadian River, and Canadian by its very nature was associated with Canada.

My mind was racing. My data banks whirred and clicked as they worked through the mass of new evidence in this case.

Evidence #1. There wasn't much water in the Canadian River. It consisted mostly of . . . well, sand. Sand and tamarack brush and a scattering of mesquite trees.

Evidence #2. Up ahead, I saw a quaint foreign village built on the hills south of the river. Obviously this was no ordinary town in the Texas Panhandle.

Evidence #3. I searched my data banks for information about Canada and came up with . . . cold. Canada was a cold place, right? Snow, ice, penguins, the whole nine yards.

I turned to my assistant. "Drover, does it seem cold to you?"

"Well . . . about like it was before."

"Just as I suspected. All at once it seems very cold."

"Well, that's not . . ."

"Don't try to deny the facts, Drover. It's cold back here."

"Yeah, but . . . I guess it is kind of cold."

"See? There we are. Suddenly we're both aware of the frigid cold. Okay, next point. How much do you know about Canada?"

"Well . . . they make ginger ale."

"Yes, yes? Go on. I think we're getting close to something. What else do you know about Canada?"

"Well, let me think here. They make geese."

"More, Drover, keep pushing."

"And it's . . . oh my gosh, it's . . . cold in Canada."

I gave him a triumphant smile. "There we have it, Drover. Unless I'm badly mistaken, we have just entered the distant foreign land of Canada."

All at once he covered his eyes with his front paws. "Oh my gosh, I knew it, help, take me home!"

"But to confirm this, we'll need a few more pieces of evidence. Uncover your eyes and go into Data Gathering Mode."

He did, and we both began searching the country around us for clues. We crossed the long bridge and entered the outskerps of town. There, Drover saw something.

"There's a clue. It's a rodeo arena."

I studied on that one. "I'm sorry, son, but that doesn't fit our pattern. Keep looking."

"There's one. Look, that sign says . . . 'Canadian City Limits.'"

I focused on the sign, and sure enough, Drover was right. "Good shot, Drover, that was a bull's-eye. The evidence is mounting up, isn't it? Now, to confirm our theory, we need one final clue."

"I want to go home!"

"Hush, Drover, concentrate. This could be very important to this case. What we're looking for now, the last piece in this puzzle, is . . . we need to find a penguin."

He stared at me. "A penguin?"

"Yes, a penguin. Don't give me that loony expression. If this is Canada and if Canada is cold, we will find evidence of penguins."

"I'll be derned."

Just then . . . "Aha! Look there, Drover, on the side of the road."

He looked. "It's a black-and-white dog."

"It's a black-and-white penguin."

"It sure looks like a dog to me."

"It's a penguin. That just about wraps it up, son. We are in Canada for sure." Just then the penguin ran out into the street and followed our pickup. And he seemed to be . . . hmm. "Drover, have you ever heard of a penguin barking at a pickup?"

"Not really."

"Me neither. He certainly sounds like a dog, doesn't he? And now that I study his overall bodily conformation, he even looks a bit like a dog, wouldn't you say?" I whirled around and faced him—Drover, that is. "Drover, what we have here is a barking dog, not a penguin."

"That's what I said. At least, I think that's what I said."

"Which means that our whole house is a theory of cards, and it may have just come crashing down around us. I don't want to alarm you, Drover, but this may not be Canada after all."

"You mean . . ."

"Exactly. As of this very moment, we have no idea where we are. All we know for sure is that they don't have penguins here."

"This leg is killing me!"

I was in the midst of feeling very discouraged. I mean, after working so hard to amass and fit together all the clues, our case was now in scrambles. But the worst was yet to come.

Do I dare reveal what happened next? I don't know, what do you think? What would you say if I told you that suddenly and all of a sudden a black-and-white police car came out of nowhere and began chasing us?

Oops, I guess I let it slip and now you know the terrible truth—that all at once we found ourselves on the wrong side of the law, common crinimals who were being chased and pursued by a speeding police car with its lights flashing!

Pretty scary, huh? You bet it was. Maybe you think it was just the black-and-white dog chasing us and not a black-and-white police car. Ha. We should have been so lucky. No, it was a police car, all right, and he not only had his lights flashing, but he even turned on his siren.

Drover and I exchanged worried glances. After a moment, he broke the icy silence. "Gosh, what did we do?"

"I don't know, son, but this is looking very serious. Did you happen to see the name on the side of that car? It said 'Canadian Police.'"

"Oh my gosh, the Mounties?"

"Yes, we're about to be arrested by the Mounties."

"But I thought we weren't in Canada."

"It's confusing, isn't it? Even I'm confused, Drover, and that's a sure sign that things have gotten out of control. Quick, we've got to hide."

We pressed ourselves into the left front corner of the pickup bed. And we waited to find out why and how we had landed on the Ten Most Wanted Dogs list of the Royal Canadian Mounted Police.

My life passed before my very eyes—a happy childhood, a long and glorious career as Head of Ranch Security, a few tiny mistakes here and there. Then it hit me.

"Drover, I've just figured it out. I know why they're after us."

"Oh my gosh, you mean . . ."

"Yes, exactly. Do you remember the day Sally May put those steaks out to thaw on the back porch?"

"Well, let's see here . . ."

"They vanished, remember? I told you they were probably stolen by a chicken hawk, remember? Well, that was a small lie."

"You mean . . ."

"Yes. I did it. I stole them in daily broadlight. I couldn't resist, I couldn't help myself, I became a victim of this . . . this terrible urge, and yes, Drover, I STOLE THE STEAKS!"

"Yeah, but that was months ago."

"But you're forgetting one small detail: they were Sally May's steaks. She never forgets anything, she holds a grudge for years and years."

"So you think . . ."

"Yes. She turned us in to the Mounties, and now the chickens have come home to rot. We may spend the rest of our lives behind bars—all because you failed me in my hour of greatest need!"

"Yeah, but I didn't eat 'em."

"But you did something worse, Drover. You knew I had a fatal weakness for steaks and you didn't stop me."

"I wasn't even there!"

"That's my whole point. If you'd been there . . ."

We felt the pickup slowing down. We exchanged glances with big moon-shaped eyes. Or to put it more accurately, Drover's eyes were moon-shaped, and although I couldn't actually see my own eyes, I had every reason to think they were every bit as moon-shaped as Drover's.

We heard the crunch of loose gravel as the pickup pulled over to the side of the road. The pickup came to a stop. Slim shut off the engine. The Mountie shut off his siren. A deadly silence moved over us. Then . . .

CHAPTER SIX

We Are Arrested by the Canadian Mounties

I heard the sound of a car door opening, then the sound of the door as it slammed shut. The crackle of the police radio. Footsteps approaching the pickup.

My mouth was dry. I felt needles of fear moving down my spine bone and out to the end of my tail. The long arm of Sally May had finally caught up with me.

Us, I should say. The long arm of Sally May had finally caught up with us.

I turned to Drover. "Drover, no matter what happens here, I want you to know that this was mostly your fault. If you'd been a true friend, you would have told me to leave those steaks alone."

He was almost in tears by now. "All these weeks and months I've felt so guilty about something, and now I know what it was! I feel terrible!"

"I understand, and if it would make you feel better to take the rap for this, I guess that would be all right with me."

"Yeah, but I don't want to go to jail!"

"You should have thought of that months ago. Part of growing up and becoming a mature dog is accepting the consequences of my own behavior. I'm sorry."

"But what about my leg?"

"You'll just have to take it to jail with you. And always remember . . ."

I wasn't able to give Drover his Lesson for the Day, because . . .

The footsteps drew closer and closer. I could hear our hearts and livers pounding. We dogs closed our eyes and waited to hear those dreaded words that would change our lives forever: *Come out with your hands up! In the name of the Royal Canadian Mounted Police, you dogs are under arrest!*

But you know what? That's not what we heard. What we heard was, "Morning. May I see your driver's license please?"

And then Slim's voice said, "Shore. Let me see,

it's s'posed to be here in my wallet . . . good honk, there's that rodeo ticket I couldn't find two years ago. Here we are."

Officer: "Thank you. Slim, is this your current address?"

Slim: "Well, it was until about an hour ago. I sort of retired from my ranch job and was on my way to Alpine. Thought I might find some cowboy work down there."

Officer: "I see. Well, Slim, I've got some bad news."

Slim: "Uh-oh. What did I do this time?"

Officer: "Well, the taillights don't work on your pickup."

Slim: "I've been meaning to . . ."

Officer: "And the tag's expired."

Slim: "Oops."

Officer: "And your inspection sticker expired two years ago."

Slim: "The same year I lost my ticket to the rodeo. Boy, time gets away, don't it?"

Officer: "So you're driving a vehicle that's about as illegal as it can be. I guess you won't be going to Alpine for a while."

Slim: "Do they feed good at the jail?"

Officer: "Ha. There's no need for that, but dang it, Slim, if you're going to drive a vehicle on

Texas highways, you've got to follow the rules."

Slim: "Yes sir, I know you're right, but I've got a little problem. I've got just enough cash to buy gas to Alpine, and that's it."

Officer: "Well . . . that's a problem, sure enough. I guess you'd better park this thing here in Canadian and find a job. With fines and fees, you're going to need about a hundred bucks—and that's with me giving you warning tickets instead of citations."

Slim: "I'm mighty grateful."

The officer spent the next ten minutes writing out Slim's warning tickets. Slim didn't say a word. Neither did we dogs. We kept still, even though I was feeling a whole lot better about this deal. Do you see what this meant? Sally May hadn't sent the law after us after all, and we wouldn't be spending the rest of our lives behind bars! Boy, what a relief.

Well, the officer wrote out the tickets and handed them to Slim and said, "Well, are you planning a big Christmas?"

"Oh yeah. Huge. Thanks, officer. I'll park this thing, like you said."

"Fine. Oh, and Slim, if you're going to be in town for a spell, I'd advise you to get tags for your dogs."

"Dogs? What dogs?"

Slim opened the door and stepped out. All at once we noticed . . . that is, we became aware of his, uh, face peering over the edge of the pickup bed. He didn't look very happy, to tell you the truth, and all at once I felt a powerful urge to . . . well, switch my tail over to Slow Whaps. And I squeezed up a little smile that said, "Hey, Slim. Bad day, huh? Well, at least you've got us dogs."

The officer got into his car and drove away. Slim stood there for several minutes, shaking his head and moving his lips. Then he turned his glare back on us.

"You birdbrains. Didn't I have enough trouble without y'all . . . oh brother. Loper probably thinks I stole his dogs."

He looked so pitiful, I hopped out of the pickup and went to him. He reached down a hand and stroked me on the ears. "Didn't I tell y'all you couldn't come? See, I had to leave the ranch. They couldn't afford to keep a hired man on the place but they didn't have the heart to fire me. I just couldn't stand the thought of being a burden. Now you've made a mess and . . . and I don't know what to do."

He stood there for a long time, shaking his head and talking under his breath while cars and trucks whizzed by on the highway. He sure looked lost and alone. I jumped up on him and nuzzled my face into his hands.

At last he spoke. "Now, here's the way it looks to me. I'm gonna have to live in this pickup until I can find me some work. I'll find a pay phone and call Loper and tell him about you dogs. Now we're cookin'. We've got us a plan." He hitched up his jeans and looked down at me. "Well, let's load up. I guess we're gonna be together for a while, for better or worse. Get in the back, Hank."

I jumped into the back and joined Mister Moon Eyes. "Drover, at last I've got this thing worked out. Listen closely so that I don't have to repeat myself."

"What?"

"I said, repeat this closely so that I don't have to listen to myself. Are you ready?"

"I guess."

"Okay. We were on our way to the Alpine Alps but we didn't make it because Slim meant to do something but didn't. We're in Canadian but that has nothing to do with Canada. Is that clear?"

"Not really. What about all those penguins and Mounties?"

"They were fignewtons of your imagination." The pickup lurched out into the street, throwing us toward the back. "Any more questions?"

"What about Sally May's steaks?"

Slim put in the clutch and shifted gears, which threw us against the cab.

"They're still missing, Drover, and we've gone back to our original theory. They must have been stolen by a chicken hawk, a sneaking, thieving chicking hawk."

"Oh good. The guilt was about to get me down."

Slim shifted again, throwing us toward the back.

I raised my voice over the roar of the engine. "I wish he'd learn to drive this thing! It's hard for a dog to carry on an intelligent conversation back here!"

He slammed on his brakes and sent us tumbling forward. I found myself standing nose-to-nose with Drover.

He grinned. "Oh, hi. It's hard to stand up back here, isn't it?"

"Yes, it certainly is, and just for that, I think I'll lie down."

"Yeah, me too. That'll teach him."

And so it was that we lodged our protests against the driver by flopping down. That put an end to all our sloshing around and claw-scraping. It also ended our conversation, which was fine with me. I had explained our situation as clearly as I could, and it was now up to Drover to make sense of it.

Slim drove into the center of town, made a left turn at the stoplight, and drove up the main street, which was built on a steep hill. Halfway up, he tried to shift down to a lower gear but missed. The pickup chugged and died, and we began rolling backward down the hill.

I leaped to my feet and barked. "What the heck is he doing now?"

Lucky for us there weren't any cars back there, so we weren't killed in a wreck. What happened was that, after rolling back down the hill fifty feet or so, Slim slammed on his brakes, which sent me crashing nosefirst into the tail endgate. Did it hurt? You bet it did. Try it sometime and see if it doesn't hurt.

Through watering eyes, I beamed a gaze of righteous anger toward the cab. Slim stuck his head out the window and gave me a big grin. "Hang on, dogs! We'll give 'er one more try." He stuffed the gear shift lever up into grandma low, and off we went.

At this point, the G-forces became so powerful they caused Drover to come sliding down to the endgate. He gave me his patented silly grin. "Oh, hi. We move around a lot, don't we?"

"Yes, and I'll tell you something else, Drover. Sometimes I get the feeling that Slim doesn't show us the proper respect when we ride in the back. He may even be doing it on purpose. Can you believe a grown man would show so little respect to his dogs?"

"Yeah, and he's lucky to have us."

"He certainly . . ." By then, we had made it to the top of the hill. Slim pulled into a parking spot in front of the courthouse . . . and would you like to guess what he did? *He slammed on his stupid brakes* and sent me flying against the cab again! Drover was still sitting, and he slid all the way to the front.

Okay, that did it. I was outraged. When he stepped out of the cab, I met him with a glare of purest steel. I wanted him to know what I thought of his childish, infantile behavior.

Do you think he took the hint—that it's hard for a dog to maintain his dignity when he's staggering around in the back of his own pickup? Do you think he showed even the smallest shred of shame or remorse? Ha.

Would you like to hear what he said? Here it is, word for word.

He said, "Pooch, if you're gonna be a ranch dog, you need to learn how to ride in the back of a pickup." And then he chuckled.

He thinks he's so funny. Well, he's not. It would have served him right if I had . . . but then he tore off a piece of beef jerky and pitched it to me, and what the heck, he wasn't such a bad guy after all. I caught it in midair and wolfed it down.

I won't say that the jerky totally healed my wounded pride, but it helped a bunch. One of us had to show some maturity in these deals, and as long as the supply of jerky held out, I figured I could handle it.

Slim Finds
a New Career

$\overline{}$

Pretty good stuff, that jerky. Did you know that Slim made his own? He did. He cut the meat up into strips, sprinkled it with his own blend of spices, and . . .

HOT PEPPER?

Suddenly my mouth was in flames and my eyes were watering.

What kind of moron would ruin a piece of jerky by covering it with . . . that stuff was burning my mouth up! I began pawing at my mouth, trying to get the flames away from my tongue and lips. My eyes were watering, my nose was running, my whole mouth and tongue and lips were being consumed by a raging fire.

Slim chuckled. "I call that my Range Fire Jerky, pooch. What do you think?"

I thought . . . I thought that was the worst garbage I'd ever had in my mouth, and I should have known better than to eat anything made by a bachelor cowboy, and he sure as thunder didn't need to worry about ME trying to steal any of his . . .

He pitched a piece of it in Drover's direction. Just for a moment, I forgot all my pain and so forth and prepared myself for some fun. He's a gulper, you know, Drover is. He'll gulp down any old thing, eats like a hog, only this time the little dunce sniffed it and crawled off into a corner.

Slim shook his head. "Dumb dog." And then he walked up to the courthouse to buy a newspaper.

Never eat any of Slim's jerky.

And don't ride in the back of his pickup either.

I had terrible indigestion for the rest of the day, but that's not why Slim bought the newspaper. He bought it to see if there were any ranch jobs listed in the classified ads.

He let down the tail endgate and used it for a seat, spread out the paper, and frowned over the classified section. The longer he read, the deeper his frown became. At last he raised up, pushed his hat to the back of his head, and said, "Boys, with this dadgum cattle market like it is, ranch jobs are as scarce as hen's teeth. Man alive, I don't know . . ."

Then his eye fell on something on the page. He leaned down and squinted at it. "I'll be derned. Lookie here. It's an ad for Leonard's Saddle Shop. You don't reckon old Leonard moved his shop over to Canadian, do you? Heck, it's just right down the street. Might be worth a try."

His expression darkened as he looked at us. What was the deal? What had we done? We'd just been sitting there like perfect dogs . . . with our mouths on fire. Or my mouth. Drover had managed to dodge that bullet, so he'd been staring at the clouds.

But the point is, Slim had no reason to be glaring at us. But he was.

"Now dogs, I'm going to hike down to Leonard's Saddle Shop. If y'all can act halfway civilized, I'll take you with me, but you've got to mind and be good, hear?"

Drover and I traded glances, and I whapped my tail several times. No problem. We took a solemn oath to be Dogs That Would Make Our Master Proud. I mean, who wants to sit in the back of a pickup when there are exciting places to explore? Not me, and if the price for going was to be a perfect, obedient dog, I was ready to give it a shot.

And besides, he hadn't actually said we had to be perfect. He'd said, and this is a direct quote, he'd said we had to "act halfway civilized." You bet, no problem.

And so we set out walking down the hill, looking into every store window and checking out all the sights of town. Drover and I followed behind Slim. I mean, you'd have thought we were a couple of those high-dollar border collies that have been to college and stuff.

We hadn't gone far when we passed a pay phone on the curb. Slim stopped, snapped his fingers, and walked over to it. "Almost forgot, I need to call Loper and tell him where his dogs are. And I wonder how his deal with the banker went. Probably not so good."

He dug into his jeans pocket and came out with a quarter. He dropped it into the slot, listened to the jingle it made, and dialed the number. He waited. And waited. A scowl gathered on his brow, and the longer he waited, the deeper and darker it got. He held the receiver away from his ear and said something to it, then slammed it down in the holder.

He waited for his quarter to come back, but it didn't. I could see that he was getting mad. He rattled the receiver and banged on the box. The quarter didn't come back, and by now he was really steamed. His eye fell on a piece of paper lying in the gutter. He stomped over to it, snatched it up, wrote a message on it with a ballpoint pen, and fixed it to the phone, where everyone could see it. It said:

"THIS PHONE IS A LIAR AND A THEEF, IT STOLD A QUARTER FROM A UNUMPLOYED COWBOY WHO NEEDED IT!!!!!!"

He stepped back and read his work, then shot a glance at us dogs. "There, by grabs, that'll teach 'em."

We continued our walk down the street, until we came to a store window that said "Leonard's

Saddle Shop. Saddles, Ropes, Tack, Chaps, and Boot Repair. A Cowboy Place." Slim didn't go in right away. He squinted his eyes and peered into the window. It was fairly dark inside and he didn't see anyone, so he paced for a while and grumbled under his breath.

At last he worked up enough courage to take a harder look. He went to the glass door, cupped his hands around his eyes, and pressed his face against the glass. All at once the door flew open and there stood Leonard, a smallish man with beady little eyes, who was wearing black cowboy boots and a dirty apron.

He didn't appear too friendly at first. He glared at us dogs, then at Slim, and a crooked smile formed on his lips. "Well, I knew it was a country fool, leaving nose prints on my front door." He wiped the glass door with his shirt sleeve. "Howdy-doo, Slim, get yourself in here. It's been a while. Sit down there by the stove and warm your bones."

He held open the door and . . . well, he hadn't exactly invited us dogs to come in, but he hadn't told us not to, so you might say that we . . . well, made a run for the stove.

We made it through the door without any . . . okay, maybe Slim tripped over me as I went streaking between his legs, but mostly it was a slick entry. We headed straight for the big gas stove in the middle of the store, hit the floor, and assumed the curled-up positions of dogs who had, well, been there for hours—dogs who belonged in a saddle shop, just as surely as the stove belonged there.

I closed my eyes but kept my ears alert for any problems. I held my breath and waited. Slim muttered something about "almost knocked me down," but that was it. He didn't order us outside. See? I'd known all along that he'd wanted us to come in, and in exchange for that, he got our solemn pledge to be perfect dogs: no barking or wrestling, no throwing up on the floor, no crude behavior of any kind.

Slim came over and pulled up one of the chairs beside the stove. I heard it scrape across the floor, and I cracked one eye. He sat down and threw one leg over the other knee, and I noticed that he seemed to be scowling down at . . . well, me. Us. Someone down there.

"You boys are making yourselves right at home, I see."

Oh yes. Fine. Thanks. Nice stove.

Leonard closed the door and joined us at the stove. He had a sparkle in his eyes and was rubbing his hands together. "Slim, you have come in here on a good day."

"Uh-oh."

"No, now hear me out. I have some fine boots I need to sell, and it is clear to me that you need a pair of my fine boots."

"What ever gave you that idea?"

"The duct tape, Slim. It don't match the color of your boots. Now, I have some Sanders bullhides that will fit you like a glove, and I can feel a weakness coming over me, even as we speak. If you was to offer me seventy bucks . . ."

"Ain't got it, Leonard."

"Sixty bucks."

"Can't handle it."

Leonard scowled. "How about a new rope?" Slim shook his head. "A cinch webbing?" He threw a glance at us. "What do you call them dogs?"

"Eat and Sleep."

Leonard laughed. "That's good. Now, about that new pair of boots . . ."

Slim shook his head. "Leonard, I've fell on hard times." And he told Leonard all the things that had happened to us that day. "So here I am in Canadian—broke, no job, no place to stay. All I've got to my name is these two dogs, and they ain't even my dogs."

Leonard chewed his lip. "Slim, do you know what you need?"

"Sure. A rich widder woman with a forty-section ranch, eight hundred oil wells, and a yellow Cadillac."

"Ha! Well, yes, who don't? But what you really need, son," he reached over and poked Slim on the arm, "is a nice little job."

"I know, but I already checked the paper. Nothing."

Leonard studied his fingernails. "Well now, it might depend on what you're willing to do. I agree, the cowboy work is scarce right now. Timing's wrong. It's winter and the cattle market's bad. But there might be other things."

"Such as?"

Leonard arched his brows and folded his hands across his chest. "You won't like it. I mean, I know you Slim, I know your breed. I used to be a cowboy myself, and if it couldn't be done a-horseback, I wouldn't do it. Am I right?"

"Well . . . I've had them thoughts, yes, but that was before this deal come up. Did you have something in mind?"

Leonard walked past the counter and went to the back of the shop. He stopped at a workbench and started cutting out a piece of leather. "Naw, you wouldn't do it. You've got too much of that cowboy pride."

Slim pushed himself up and walked to the counter. "Never mind the cowboy pride. Keep talking."

"Well, sir, how would you feel about . . . cleaning out a chicken house?"

Slim's brows jumped, and he swallowed so hard his Adam's apple did a flip. He walked to the front window and stared out, then he walked back to the counter. "It's what I've always dreamed of doing, Leonard. Since I was a boy, I've wanted to clean out a chicken house." Leonard barked a laugh. "But I need a place to sleep, and I ain't too keen on sleeping in a chicken house."

Leonard wiped his hands on his apron and came striding over to the counter. "I've got this little place on the edge of town, keep my horse Billy there, you know, and it's got an old chicken house. Now, my wife's got it in her head to start raising fryers again and she's been after me to clean out the chicken house. Naturally, I've found fifty-two reasons why I can't do it. What do you say?"

"Does it come with a bed?"

"It's got a house, cute little house, just perfect for you and them dogs."

"What does that mean?"

Leonard looked up at the ceiling. "Well, it ain't exactly a house."

"What exactly is it?"

"A camper trailer, Slim, and just as cute as a button. You'll love it."

Slim stared at the floor. "A camper trailer. Does it have a inside pot?"

"It's got a mayonnaise jar on the inside and a one-hole johnny on the outside, and Slim, that's all a man like you needs." Leonard came around the counter, put his hand on Slim's shoulder, and started easing him toward the door. "It'll take you a couple days. I'll pay you a hundred bucks and grub. I'll even furnish the shovel and wheelbarrow. What a deal, huh?"

"Well . . ."

"And if you decide to blow your wages on boots, I'll make you a heck of a swap." By that time they had reached the door. Leonard reached around Slim and opened it. "Here's twenty bucks. Get yourself some grub at the grocery store. When you're done, come by and we'll settle up." He gave Slim a pat on the shoulder and pushed him toward the door.

"Yeah, but Leonard . . ."

"Let me know how that indoor pot works. And don't forget to feed my horse."

And with that, Slim left the store—leaving us dogs inside!

CHAPTER EIGHT

Survivest
of the Fiddles

You'll be relieved to know that Slim didn't leave us in Leonard's Saddle Shop. He stood outside a moment, then stuck his head back inside.

"Leonard, maybe you'd better tell me where this place is located."

Leonard snapped his fingers and strode over to the counter and dashed off some directions. He handed them to Slim and pushed him out the door again. When Slim was gone, he shook his head and sighed. "That boy's got tar in his veins." Just then, he saw us sitting by the stove. He ran to the door. "Hey! You forgot your dogs."

Slim shrugged, turned around, and came back inside. "Well, you're so dadgum pushy, you made me forget. Come on, dogs, we'll take our business somewhere's else."

"Right. Take your business to my worst enemy."

We dogs went slinking past him. We slinked . . . slank . . . whatever . . . because we didn't trust the guy. Sure enough, as we went by, he made kind of a monkey face at me. I growled and sprinted out the door.

Outside on the street, Slim looked up at the winter clouds and heaved a deep sigh. "Boys, I've sunk about as low as a cowboy can sink. I sure wish I had my old job back."

He shoved his hands into his pockets, kicked a rock out into the street, and we trudged back up the hill to the pickup. We dogs loaded into the back and Slim drove to a little grocery store down the street. He emerged fifteen minutes later, carrying a sack of groceries in one arm and a sack of dog food in the other, and we resumed our journey.

Slim found Leonard's place in the country, but it wasn't so easy. It was north and east of town, out in the middle of that heavy tamarack brush in the old river bottom. To reach it, we followed a winding two-track trail through the brush, and when the trail ended, we were there.

Slim got out and turned up the collar of his jacket. The wind had shifted to the north, gray clouds had moved overhead, and there was a feel of snow in the air. He dug his hands into his pockets and walked to the . . . uh . . . house. The trailer. The "cute little camper trailer."

It resembled a tin can on two wheels, and both tires were flat. A long yellow extension cord ran from a utility pole, through a hole in the side, and into the house. That appeared to be the electrical service.

The trailer was blue. Or green. It was some faded color between blue and green, but mostly it was faded. Oh, and someone had cut a hole in the roof and run a joint of stovepipe out the top, a hint that it was heated with a wood-burning stove.

The trailer sat in a grove of chinaberry trees. The front porch consisted of a sheet of plywood perched on four cinder blocks. It wasn't much of a porch, and I certainly hoped that Slim didn't plan on us dogs sleeping on it.

Leonard's horse pen was off to the west. It appeared that he had set up eight or ten portable corral panels, tied them to chinaberry trees with baling wire, and put his haystack on the north side as a windbreak. Inside the pen stood a big bay horse. When he heard us, he turned his head for a moment, stared at us dogs, then went back to eating his alfalfa hay.

I mean, no hello, no greeting, no "welcome to the place." I had a feeling that this horse and I weren't going to be pals.

Slim opened the door of the trailer and went inside and put his sack of groceries on the counter. He didn't exactly invite us to join him, but he didn't tell us we couldn't, so . . . if they don't say no, it means yes, right? We managed to slither through his legs and make our way inside.

It was . . . small. Very small. On the west side, there was a little refrigerator and gas cooking stove, and the east wall was taken up by a couch, which probably served as the bed, since there wasn't any room for a bed. Yes, it was the bed, had to be. In the middle of the room sat the wood stove and one chair, and that was about it.

Slim ran his eyes around the place and said, "Well, it beats living in the pickup, I reckon."

We went back outside and followed Slim on a slow trudge to the place where he would be working for the next few days, the chicken house. No doubt it had once been a pretty nice affair, but time had taken its toll. The white paint and red trim had faded and cracked, the wood shingles on the roof had buckled, and the chicken yard had grown up in tall weeds.

Slim opened the door and peeked inside. So did

I. My goodness, on the dirt floor beneath the roosts there was a whole mountain range of . . . of something that smelled *really bad*. Slim slumped against the wall and fanned the fumes away from his face.

"Good honk. Five tons of chicken manure." He blinked his eyes several times and heaved a sigh. "Well, I might as well get started. I'm just glad my cowboy friends can't see me now."

He found the wheelbarrow and shovel and went to work. He parked the wheelbarrow in the chicken house door and shoveled it full, then pushed it out to the edge of the tamaracks and dumped it. Then back to the chicken house for another load. Back and forth, back and forth, until the sun went down. When it got too dark for work, he parked the wheelbarrow and went to the house.

It had started snowing by then, and when we reached the trailer I was pretty sure that Slim would want us to stay inside, so once again, Drover and I were . . . well, plotting our Rapid Entry, so to speak. When Slim's hand closed around the doorknob, I was poised and ready to spring into action.

I waited and watched him out of the corner of my eye. The enormous muscles in my legs were coiled like springs. The doorknob squeaked, and when I saw a shaft of light streaming through the crack in the door, I timed my jump perfectly so that . . .

BONK!

He didn't open the door. He *faked it*, knowing full well that I would . . . what a dirty trick! He chuckled, but I didn't think it was very funny, not at all. I looked up at him and gave him Puzzled Wags on the tail section.

"Hank, you've just about knocked me down three times today, squirting through doors. Maybe you'd better stay outside and think about your manners. Besides, this tin can ain't big enough for three of us."

Drover and I traded glances. I gave him the sign to switch over to Tragic Eyes. He did and I did, and in a matter of mere seconds, we had switched all circuits over to Tragic Eyes, Disappointed Ears, and Mournful Wags. We beamed these earnest messages to Slim, in hopes that . . .

"No, you can't make me feel guilty. I'm gripey and cold-hearted and I've been scooping chicken hockey for the past three hours, so I ain't in my usual sweet frame of mind. Y'all just spend the night out here on the porch. Nightie-night."

And with that, he went into the trailer and slammed the door in our faces, leaving us alone

with our broken hearts. Oh, and with a bunch of snowflakes too.

I turned to Drover. "What a heartless cad he turned out to be."

"Yeah, I thought we did pretty well with Tragic Eyes."

"We did very well, Drover. We've never done it better, and it should have worked. I don't know what's wrong with him."

"Well . . . I guess you tripped him a couple of times today, going through doors. I saw it myself."

I glared at the runt. "Well yes, I guess you did—since you were right there beside me, pushing and shoving and being Mister Buttinski. When you push and shove and display your terrible manners, what am I supposed to do?"

"Well . . . I guess you could let me go first."

"Let you go . . . oh brother, now I've heard everything! Let you go first? Ha! Drover, that's the . . . do you have any idea what would happen if I let you go first?"

"Well, let me think." He rolled his eyes around. "Nope, I don't know."

"I'll tell you." I stood up and began pacing back and forth on the tiny plywood porch. "If I started allowing you to enter houses before me, it would . . . it would corrupt you in small but tiny ways. You'd start grabbing the best spots around the stove and the softest places on the floor. You'd get soft and flabby. You'd become a greedy, grabby little mutt, overbearing and insensitive to the needs of others. Is that what you want in this life?"

"Well . . . it might be fun to try it."

I stopped pacing and stared into his greedy, grabby little eyes. "I can't believe you said that."

"Yeah, but I did. It just . . . popped out."

"Okay, fine. If that's the way you want it, if you insist on ignoring all my efforts and sacrifices, by George, we'll just try it your way. And we'll just see what happens."

"Oh goodie."

"The next time this comes up, we'll turn you loose. We'll let you transform yourself into a greedy grabber. We'll let you grevel and rovvel in your own corrupt behavior. We'll let you . . ."

At that very moment my lecture was cut short by the opening of the door. Slim stepped out, booted us off the so-called porch, and spread out a saddle blanket. "There. My conscience is now clear. See you boys in the morning." And he went back inside.

The moment the door slammed behind him, and I mean, the very instant . . . guess what happened. Drover leaped onto the blanket, staked out the very choicest spot in the middle, and flopped down.

"What are you doing?"

He gave me a silly grin. "Well, we decided to let me go first and I did, and you know what? I kind of enjoyed it."

I stepped up on the porch and showed him some fangs. "Scram. You're on my spot."

"Yeah but . . . we said . . . you said . . ."

"We were talking about doors and houses, Drover. This is a blanket. Do you know the difference between a door and a blanket and a house?"

"Well, let me think. Seventeen?"

"No, that's totally incorrect. The difference is twenty-three, and I hope you realize the significance of that number."

"I guess I don't."

"There, you see? I'm sorry, Drover, but until you understand the meaning of your own meaningless behavior, I must insist on getting first dibs on all blankets. Now move."

He moaned and grumbled, but he moved. I took my rightful position in the middle of the blanket, circled it three times, and flopped down. Drover curled up on the west edge, where he continued to moan, grumble, and complain.

"Everything's so complicated. And I'm cold."

"Hush, Drover. It's cold only if you believe it's cold. Pretend that you're living in the desert. Good night."

He curled up in a little white ball and began . . . shivering. I tried to ignore the fact that my bed was quivering, but after a while, it began getting on my nerves.

I raised my head. "Will you stop shivering? How can a dog sleep when his bed feels like Jell-O?"

"I can't help it. I'm f-f-freezing."

"That's too bad. We've been forced to sleep outside. It's survivest of the fiddles."

"Yeah, but I can't even carry a tune."

"That's fine, Drover, because we're not singing. Now go to sleep and stop shivering."

And so it was that we settled in for a cold night on the porch.

CHAPTER NINE

We're Freezing Our Tails!

All went well for a couple of minutes. Then I felt the bed shaking again. I lifted my head and looked over at Drover. "Are you shivering again?"

"Well, I don't think so. I'm about to freeze, but I've been trying extra hard not to shiver."

"That's odd. I'm almost sure I felt the bed . . . hmmm. I seem to be shivering. It's cold, isn't it?"

"Yeah, and I think it's getting c-c-c-colder by the minute. You reckon we ought to pile on top of each other to stay warm?"

"No. Absolutely not. Go to sleep." I thought about the piling-on deal for a moment. "Actually, that's not such a bad idea. Our bodies could share their warmth."

"Yeah, and sharing's part of good manners."

"Good point. Okay, we'll try it, but I'm on top."

"Okay with me, 'cause it's warmer on the bottom."

I studied him for a moment. "Which is why I'm taking the bottom."

"I thought you wanted the top."

"I was misquoted, Drover. You must beware of misquoting others and leaping to conclusions."

He raised himself and plopped down on top of me. Ooof. He was heavier than you might have supposed, but also pretty warm. I figured I could stand it for one night. I closed my eyes, shifted my breathing control over to the Slow and Deep setting, and drifted off into . . . a foot in my face?

"Drover, get your foot out of my face this very minute."

"Murgle skiffer porkchop faceless footies rickie tattoo."

I spun my legs for several seconds, until I got a firm grip on the porch. Then I heaved myself upward and threw him off my back. When he sat up, his ears were crooked.

"Drover, this isn't working. I can't sleep with your foot in my face all night. I guess we'll have to . . . wait a minute, wait just a minute! I've got an idea, and I think this one will work."

I began pacing back and forth in front of the

runt, as I often do when a brilliant idea begins taking rot in the vast fields of my mind. Taking *root*, I should say.

"I've got it, Drover. Here's the deal. We'll sing our way into the house. We've done it before, maybe it'll work one more time."

"Yeah, but I still can't carry a tune, and this is survivest of the fiddles, you already said so."

"Never mind the fiddles. We don't need fiddles for this. We'll do it with our own voices, and we're going to attack his heart."

"You mean . . . give him a heart attack?"

"No, no, you don't understand. We're going to sing a song so sad and full of tragedy, it will penetrate into the deepest bones of his heart."

"I'd rather penetrate his house."

"That comes next, Drover. First we win the heart, then we win the house."

"Yeah, but we don't have a song. I'm so cold, the only song I can remember is 'Three Blind Ducks.'"

"It's 'Three Blind Mice.'"

"I don't know that one."

"It doesn't matter, Drover. I've got the song. All we have to do is belt it out. Stand by for Heavy Duty Singing."

We parked ourselves right in front of the door and shivered and moaned and beamed our most pathetic looks toward the house. Here's how it went.

We're Freezing Our Tails

Slim, we're well aware that you're cozy in
    your shack,
Reading *Western Horseman* and preparing
    for the sack.
You're drinking a hot chocolate, your feet are
    warm and dry
'Cause you held them to the stove until they
    were 'bout to fry.

We dogs are very glad that the cold has lost
    its sting,
You're sitting in your castle like a pampered
    cowboy king.
We know that you worked hard today,
    outside in wind and snow,
But there's one more little thing we think
    you really ought to know.

We're freezing, we're freezing, we're
    freezing our tails.
My derriere's frozen as stiff as a nail.
The snowdrifts grow deeper, the wind
    blows a gale.

We're freezing, we're freezing, we're
    freezing our tails.

Slim, we're well aware that you're not the
    kind of guy
Who'd harm a helpless creature or even
    kill a fly.
We know that you would worry if you found
    a homeless mouse,
Could we talk about the chances of our
    staying in your house?

We know a guilty conscience is very hard
    to bear.
It worries us most deeply that you're sitting
    in your chair,
Consumed with guilty feelings, contemplating
    all your sins,
'Cause your dogs are shaking on the porch,
    just begging to get in.

We're freezing, we're freezing, we're
    freezing our tails.
My derriere's frozen as stiff as a nail.
The snowdrifts grow deeper, the wind
    blows a gale.
We're freezing, we're freezing, we're
    freezing our tails.

Yes, we belted it out, right there on the porch, and also added some world-class howling and moaning to add to the overall effect. About halfway through the song, I noticed Slim's face at the window. Then, just as we were winding up the last chorus, the door popped open and he stuck his head out.

"Is this likely to go on all night?" Drover and I nodded our heads. "Is there anything I could do, short of killin' y'all, that would cut down on the noise?" Oh yes, just . . . let us in the, you know . . . house. That simple.

Slim heaved a sigh. "You knotheads. Okay, come on in, only we ain't . . ." We flew into the house. ". . . going to make a habit of this, and don't get on the furniture."

Furniture? Ha. No problem. There wasn't any furniture.

Shucks, this was real luxury. We had a cowhide rug on the floor and a nice woodstove to keep us warm. Was there more to life than this? I didn't think so.

Slim flopped into his chair and opened up his Ben K. Greene book and started reading. Drover curled up into a ball and went right to sleep. I flopped down . . . hmm, and noticed a wrinkle in the cowhide, right where my shoulder was resting.

I wiggled around and tried to smooth it out.

That didn't work, so I went through the entire Jack Up and Rise procedure, got to my feet, and began digging on the wrinkle. I did this as quietly as possible but Slim must have heard it. His eyes came over the top of his book.

"Hank, don't be diggin' up Leonard's carpet."

Fine. No problem. If that's the way he felt about it, I would take what was offered and suffer in silence. Or at least until he went to bed, heh heh.

Around nine-thirty he yawned and put his book aside, rose from the chair, and announced, "This excitement has wore me out. After I visit Mrs. Murphy, I'll be ready for some serious wintertime sleepin'."

He pulled on his boots and coat and went outside. Drover slept through all this, but I didn't. I had picked up some clues about the mysterious "Mrs. Murphy," don't you see, and I was curious to know just who she was and what she did around here. I went to the window, hopped up on my back legs, and peered out into the darkness.

Hmm, yes. Through squinted eyes, I observed . . . well, a rusted window screen was about all I could see. I mean, it was so old and corroded, you could hardly see out of it. The only other window on that side of the trailer was just above Slim's couch-bed.

Did I dare trespass on the bed to get a look outside? He had, after all, said something about . . . "staying off the furniture."

Hmm. On the other hand, I really needed to know about this Mrs. Murphy character. If this was going to be our home, even on a temporary basis, it was pretty important for me to know who came and went, right? Some dogs get serious about guarding the house and some don't. It was pretty clear that Drover didn't, but I sure did. To me, guarding the house was a serious and heavy responsibility, and yes, I had to know who she was, this elusive mysterious Mrs. Murphy.

I leaped up onto the bed, parted a set of dusty little curtains with my nose, and peered out into the night. At first I saw nothing and no one.

Then, all of a sudden, I saw a strange man come out of a . . . well, some type of small narrow shed or building just beyond the horse pen. I hadn't noticed it before. It sat in the chinaberry grove. It had a slanted roof and a door that took up most of the east side. I mean, this was a very small shed, just barely large enough to hold one man.

And who was that guy coming out? He wore cowboy clothes but no hat. That was a pretty important clue right there. No normal cowboy would be out in this cold weather without his hat.

I made a mental note of this. I had a feeling that it might be crucial later in the investigation.

This man, this strange man who had come out of the shed, appeared to be walking toward our trailer. I felt the hair rising on my back, and a growl began to rumble in the depths of my throat. The pieces of this puzzle were falling into place, all too well and all too soon, and it was beginning to look pretty bad. Are you keeping a list of clues? Maybe not, so let me list them.

Clue #1: Slim was nowhere in sight.

Clue #2: A strange hatless man was approaching the house.

Clue #3: Most worrisome of all, Mrs. Murphy was obviously hiding somewhere. Was she lurking behind the chinaberry trees, or was it possible that she had taken refuge in the shed? And who was she? A spy, no doubt, an enemy spy who had been sent to . . . do something.

At this point, we had many questions and very few answers. What we did have was plenty of reason to move into Alert Stage One.

"Drover, wake up. I don't want to alarm you, but a strange man is approaching the house."

His head came up, one ear up and the other sagging. "Did someone call my name?"

"Yes, I did. Now listen carefully. There's a

strange man approaching the house. He will be at the door in less than ten seconds. Slim has disappeared without a trace. We don't know what happened to him, but we suspect that Mrs. Murphy had something to do with it. If the stranger comes into the house, we have no escape route. We may have to fight to the death."

That got his attention. His eyes ballooned. "Fight to the death! Oh my gosh, oh my leg, help, Mayday!"

He began squeaking and running in circles.

"Stop squeaking and bark! We've got to let this guy know that the house is being defended. Maybe if we throw up a withering barrage of barking, he'll get the message and leave."

And that's what we did. We pointed ourselves toward the door and unlooshed . . . unleashed, I guess it should be . . . unleashed our most ferocious barrage of barking. Even Drover threw himself into the effort. Once the little mutt realized the seriousness of our situation, that our backs were against the wall, he came up with some pretty good barks.

There for a minute, I thought we had stopped him—the intruder, that is—with our withering so-forths, but then I saw the doorknob turn and I heard the click of the latch.

We both stopped barking and stared at the door. I swallowed hard. "Okay, son, we gave it our best shot and it didn't work. We have no choice now but to go to Reverse Battle Stations."

I could hear his teeth chattering. "Reverse Battle Stations? What does that mean?"

"It means hide, you dunce! This is every dog for himself! Run for your life!"

In the panic that followed this announcement, Drover scrambled into a tiny space beneath the chair. This left me with no place to go, so in sheer desperation, I went into Bunker Position beneath the covers on Slim's bed.

Then in the eerie silence, we listened.

The door opened.

Footsteps entered the house.

The door slammed shut.

I could hear the pounding of my heart. In the deathly silence, it sounded like the thumping of a washtub. I could only hope that Drover didn't squeak or do anything else to give us away.

I heard the man cough. Then I heard another sound: the swish of a coat being removed and dropped upon the floor. Uh-oh, what if he planned to stay for a while? Could we maintain Radio Silence over a long period of time? It would be tough, especially for little Mister Moan and Groan.

Then suddenly a voice cut through the silence. It said, and this is an exact quote, it said, "Well, I'm back from Mrs. Murphy's."

HUH?

CHAPTER TEN

I Solve the Mystery of Mrs. Murphy, the Spy

That voice sounded very familiar, almost like . . . well, almost like Slim's voice, yet I had observed the intruder myself and had been pretty sure . . .

I summoned up the courage to lift the sheet with my nose, just enough so that I could peek out with one eye. Hmmm. It certainly appeared to be Slim, I mean, right down to the smallest details: the long pointed nose, the glasses, the belt buckle, the faded jeans that bagged in the seat.

"Get out of my bed."

Sure, okay, but . . . I slithered myself out of the sheets and off the bed and approached him in a

stealthy manner. See, we still had a lot of loose ends in this case, and I wasn't convinced that this was actually Slim. Sometimes they'll use disguises, you know, your spies and your enemy agents, and they're very clever about it.

The last thing I wanted was to come out of this deal looking foolish. I wouldn't be convinced that this was actually Slim until I got close enough to give him a thorough sniffing. I moved toward him one step at a time. I watched his face very carefully and raised the hair on my back, just in case this turned out to be a truck.

A trick, I should say.

Sniff. Sniff. Sniff.

Okay, chicken manure. You can relax. We, uh, cancelled the alert. False alarm, in other words, but let me hasten to point out that *he hadn't been wearing his cowboy hat*. That had changed his appearance entirely. I mean, what's a cowboy without a cowboy hat? They never go anywhere without a hat, and when they do . . . well, they run the risk of being mistaken for somebody else.

And if he didn't want his dogs going into a panic, he should have . . .

Never mind, just skip it.

I tapped my tail on the floor and rolled my eyes up to his face. He was shaking his head. "Good honk, I make one trip to the outhouse and you geniuses forget who I am. And stay off of my bed."

Sure, you bet, but who'd said anything about an outhouse? I thought he'd gone somewhere to hold a secret meeting with . . .

Okay, the pieces of the peezle had begun falling into place, the pieces of the puzzle. Slim was a cowboy, right? And they have their own peculiar way of communicating, right? Which always seems to involve some kind of joke, right? So instead of just making a simple statement, such as, "I'm going to visit the outhouse," he had mumbled something about "Mrs. Murphy."

Do you get it? He had his own name for the outhouse! Does that make sense? I think it's REALLY WEIRD, if you want to know what I think, and I don't know how these people expect a dog to stay on top of House Security when they're speaking in codes and leaving the house without their hats. It sure makes you think they don't take our jobs . . . oh well.

I had a little trouble getting Stub Tail out from under the chair, but finally he came creeping out. But for the rest of the evening, until the lights went out, I noticed that he was giving Slim a close inspection, just in case he turned out to be Mrs. Murphy, the spy.

I can't say that I blamed him. I mean, once these guys start playing pranks on a dog and joking around all the time, it makes you wonder. I'll say no more about it.

Well, we spent a great night inside the house, bedded down on Leonard's cowhide carpet. It was kind of fun, listening to that old north wind whistle and groan outside, whilst we were curled up beside a nice warm . . .

Oh, there was one small problem. Along about five o'clock in the morning, Slim's last load of wood had pretty muchly burned down to embers, and ... well, the house started cooling down. See, just before bedtime, he'd loaded the stove with what he'd called his "best all-nighter logs," big chunks of mesquite and hackberry that were supposed to burn through the night.

Well, they didn't quite make it, and before daylight that old floor got pretty derned cold. And hard. I awoke from a deep sleep and suddenly felt a ... a sudden and deep concern that Slim might be getting cold. Especially his feet. See, hot air rises and collects around the headatory region, while cold air falls and gathers around the feet, and the last thing we needed was for Slim to wake up with frostbitten feet.

That frostbite can be very dangerous, and you hear stories all the time about guys who were careless about the weather and got their hands and feet and ears frostbitten. You know what happens then? They have to cut 'em off. That's right, and since Slim was the breadwinner of the house, I sure as thunder didn't want to take any chances of him getting his feet sawed off.

I mean, his boots wouldn't fit anymore, and where would he put his spurs? No sir, we didn't

103

need any of that, so I took it upon myself to, uh, save his feet from the . . . frostbite hazard.

It wasn't as easy as you might think. I had to pull myself up on his bed, creep several steps to the east, and lie across his feet—all of that without waking him. See, he never would have approved of my actions. I knew that. Cowboys are proud, right? Maybe even vain. They think of themselves as tough and independent, and they never want to accept help from anyone else.

I understood all that, so I did it quietly—for his own good. I mean, if a loyal cowdog can't take care of his master's precious feet, what good is he? But this next part will really surprise you. *I didn't even take credit for it*. No sir, it was a selfless act of selfless devotion. At first light, I slithered back down on the floor and, well, shivered until Slim got the fire chunked up.

Is that touching or what? You bet it is, and you know what else? He didn't lose one foot, not even one toe, to frostbite. That just shows you what a loyal cowdog can do when he sets his mind to it. And what really surprises me is that there are people in this world who don't even own a dog. And a lot of those people are walking around without feet and toes.

Okay, where were we? Oh yes, morning. At first light Slim crept out of bed and chunked up the stove with fresh wood. Then he jumped back under the covers and grabbed another fifteen minutes of sleep. When the house warmed up, he crawled out of bed, stretched his long arms, and pushed the hair out of his face.

I lifted my head, whapped my tail on the floor, and gave him a big good morning smile. He returned it with a yawn and a scowl. "Which reminds me, I've got to call Loper and figure some way to get you dogs back to the ranch."

He made his coffee and fixed himself some breakfast. You probably think he made sausage and eggs, right? Biscuits and gravy? Ha. This guy was no chef. He was the same guy who'd made that Range Fire Jerky.

He opened a can of sardines in mustard sauce and ate it with crackers. Sardines for breakfast! He didn't offer any of it to me and Drover, and that was fine. I couldn't imagine looking a sardine in the face first thing in the morning.

We left the house around eight. It had snowed several inches in the night and little flakes were still coming down from the gray sky. Slim fed Leonard's horse, Billy, and chopped the ice on the water tank, then he opened up the sack of dog food. It was time for us to eat, it appeared, and to celebrate the moment, I went into Joyful Leaps and Vigorous Wags on the tail section.

He dipped the dog food out of the sack with an empty bean can and put it in two separate bowls, ten or fifteen feet apart. What was this? We'd always eaten out of the same bowl before.

I was all set to make a rush for the grub, but then I heard Slim's voice. "Hank! Sit."

Huh? Sit? Hey, he'd put out the grub and it was time . . .

"Sit. We're gonna work on your manners today."

Manners! Oh brother. It was a pretty boring day when Slim couldn't think of anything better to do than . . .

Okay, I sat down, but also quivered and licked my chops. Oh, and I shot a glance at Drover, just to make sure he wasn't trying to cheat. I could stand being mannerly, as long as Drover had to play by the same rules.

You've got to watch him, you know. Remember how grabby he'd been over that blanket deal? He had a pretty serious Me-First Problem and no more manners than a hog.

"Drover, sit down and wait for Slim's signal. We're doing Manners on this meal."

"Manners? How come?"

"Slim wants us to show restraint and delayed graffications."

"I'll be derned." He began scratching his ear.

"Don't scratch while I'm talking to you about manners. Scratching at mealtime is crude and rude."

"Yeah, but it feels great."

"Drover, the whole purpose of manners is to make ourselves uncomfortable. It shows a higher order of . . . something. Discipline. Restraint. It shows that we're not just dogs who eat like hogs."

"Yeah, but what's a graffication?"

"I don't know, I've never heard of it."

"You said something about it just a minute ago."

"Oh. Yes. That. Well, you've heard of graphs, I suppose, and a graffication is similar to a graph, only more so. Is that clear?" His eyes crossed. "Don't cross your eyes at me. If you don't understand something, just say so, ask a question. You don't need to make loony faces."

"Oh, okay. Can I ask a question?"

"No. If you didn't get it the first time, there's no hope that you'll get it the second or third. Just sit still and wait for the signal."

Slim finished putting out the dog food, and he noticed us sitting there like . . . well, angels. Perfect dogs. Models of good and mannerly behavior.

"Well, that's more like it. See, you hammerheads can learn a thing or two. Now, I'm going to work in the Guano Mine, so you mutts stay around the house. Don't bark at Leonard's horse, stay out of the garbage barrel, and don't wander off." He started for the chicken house, then turned around. "Oh. Y'all may eat."

He left. Thus far, I still hadn't moved toward the bowls of food, and Drover was waiting for my signal. I noticed that he was licking his chops.

"All right, Drover, I will now choose which bowl I want."

"Oh darn. How come you get to pick?"

"Because, Drover, I am older and wiser than you. For these important decisions, we must use our best minds."

"Well, mine's the best I've ever had."

"Nevertheless, I will make the choice. I hope you understand that I'm doing this for my own good."

"Oh, well, that's different. But I hope you'll hurry up."

I had no intention of hurrying up. After all, this was a very important decision.

CHAPTER ELEVEN

I Teach the Horse a Valuable Lesson

I rose from my spot and walked to the first bowl. We'll call it Bowl A. I studied the level of food kernels in the bowl and gave it a good sniffing. Then, at a leisurely pace, I walked over to the second bowl, which we'll call Bowl B. (I hope this doesn't get too complicated.) I gave it the same treatment and spent a moment thinking over my decision.

"Okay, I've decided to take Bowl A. We will now walk slowly to our respective bowls and begin eating."

"Oh good, I got the bowl I wanted."

He started toward Bowl B, but I stopped him. "Wait a minute. Why did you want Bowl B?"

"Oh, I don't know. It just looked nicer."

"Sit down, Drover, I may need to reconsider my decision." I went to Bowl B and studied it again. "You're right, this one is definitely better. I'll take it. Let's eat."

He made a dash for the Bowl A and I began munching kernels from Bowl B. They tasted . . . well, not so great, like sawdust covered with stale grease. On the other hand, Drover was making all kinds of noise over his food, which made me wonder . . .

I went back to Bowl A. "Sorry, son, I've changed my mind. I want this one."

"Yeah, but you said . . ."

"Move it. Scram, is what I said."

He ran to my bowl and I took a bite from his. Crunch, crunch. Oh yes, these kernels were much better—the taste, the texture, the . . .

I stopped chewing and raised my head. I could still hear him eating. I mean, you'd have thought he was eating a pot roast or something really special, the way he was crunching and slobbering. I found myself glaring at him. What was going on here? I had tasted the kernels from that bowl only moments before and hadn't been impressed, yet he was carrying on as if . . .

I lumbered over to Bowl A . . . Bowl B . . . whichever bowl it was, I've lost track, but I lumbered over

111

to it and pushed him aside. "Excuse me, I'm taking over here. You thought you could pull a fast one on me, huh? Sorry, pal, go back to the other bowl."

"Yeah, but I thought . . ."

I curled my lips and gave him snarl. "Now get back to your bowl and quit making a spectacle of myself."

He resumed his eating and I resumed mine. Oh yes, no question about it, the kernels in this bowl were far superior to the ones in the other. Great stuff. Much better. And just imagine, the little goof had thought he could cheat me out of the better meal!

But you know what? The more I ate of those kernels, the more they reminded me of . . . sawdust. Yet there was Drover at the next bowl, gobbling and slurping and smacking on every bite. I found myself glaring at him and wondering . . .

How could I enjoy my meal when Drover seemed to be enjoying his so much more? It didn't make any sense to me, but he sure ruined my meal, the little dunce.

After breakfast, we found warm spots on the sunny side of the house and took a nap. Wait. I took a nap and Drover took a nap. That's two naps, so I guess I should say that we found sunny so-forths and took naps—naps, plural.

I woke up an hour or two later, stood up, yawned, and stretched. Then I glanced around for something to do. Hmm, there wasn't much in the way of entertainment—no bones to chew, no chickens to scatter, no cats to run up a tree. I watched Slim push the wheelbarrow to the edge of the trees and dump it. That wasn't real exciting. At last I located a stick and chewed on it for a while.

Ho hum. I hate waiting around and being bored. It was then that I noticed Leonard's horse. Yes, Slim had said something about not barking at the horse, but I was pretty sure he wouldn't mind if I just . . . well, checked him out. No harm there, right?

Have we discussed horses? I don't like 'em, never have. Once in a while you'll find a good one, but mostly they're all the same—cocky, overbearing, and rude. I decided to drift over to the horse pen and introduce myself to this guy. What did Slim call him? Bob, I believe. No, Bill. Billy, there we go. I drifted over to the . . . I've already said that.

I sat down beside the pen and watched him eating his hay. Billy, that is, not Slim. I watched Billy the Horse eating his hay. Slim eats all kinds of awful stuff, but not hay.

Okay. It appeared to be a pretty good grade of alfalfa hay, a nice bright color of green, with plenty of leaves and not much grass or weeds. Billy took a chomp, tossed it up in the air, and sent it flying. Then he began chewing and I noticed that his eyes drifted over to me.

I had already decided to be cordial. When you're bored, really bored, being cordial to a horse can be fun. "Nice day." He went on eating. "That looks like pretty good alfalfa." Silence. "I don't eat hay myself. Is it pretty good?" Nothing.

See? What did I tell you? You speak to 'em, try to be nice, and they ignore you. I decided to try a different approach.

"You're kind of a sloppy eater, aren't you? I mean, the way you throw your food around. If I was buying your hay, I'd want you to be a little more careful with it. I hear that stuff's bringing four dollars a bale, and that doesn't include hauling and stacking."

He slouched over to the tank and took a slurp of water. He still hadn't lowered himself to speak to me, and it was beginning to grate on my nerves.

"I guess you think you're pretty hot stuff."

His head came up and several beads of water dribbled off his chin. "Yeah, I guess I do. What are you doing here?"

"I'm with Slim. We'll be here for a few days. I guess you could say that I'm Head of Ranch Security, only this isn't exactly a ranch. Ha, ha." He took another drink and didn't even smile. "Name's Hank. Hank the Cowdog. I thought it was about time we got acquainted."

He wandered over to the fence near where I was sitting. "That's nice. Now, you see this corral fence?"

"Oh yeah, it's a good stout fence. I noticed it right away."

"Uh-huh. Horses stay in here. Dogs stay outside. As long as you don't get confused about that, everything will be hunky-dory."

I gave him a sly grin. This was getting interesting. "I must have misunderstood. There for a second, I thought you were saying that the Head of Security isn't allowed in the horse pen, but that couldn't be right. I mean, it's my job to take care of the place, and unless I'm badly mistaken, this pen is part of the place."

He gazed off in the distance and sighed. "Let me say it again. Dogs outside, horses inside. It's very simple. You there, me here, no problems." He ambled back to the hay and flipped a block of it into the air.

"Yes, but suppose I need to go in there for an investigation? That might come up, you never know. Hello? I see what you're trying to do. You're trying to ignore me, but that won't work."

He didn't even look at me. Okay, fine. We'd just

see about this. I reached my left front paw under the fence and placed it in the horse pen. He didn't notice, so I scooched my other paw under the fence. That gave us a total of two dog paws in the horse pen.

Nothing happened.

Well, I was feeling bolder now and scrunched myself halfway under the fence, so that the top half of my enormous body lay inside the pen. No response. I wiggled the rest of the way through. In other words, I had just entered Forbidden Ground. How did it feel? Great. I loved it. This was turning into a pretty exciting adventure.

Billy said nothing, didn't even look my way. Okay, so I made an even bolder move. I walked five steps and waited to see what he would do about it. Ha. Nothing. He went right on munching his hay.

That's one thing I'd noticed about horses. They're so arrogant and haughty, so high and mighty, but when it comes down to action, they come up short. You know why? Laziness, just pure and simple laziness. They'll mouth off and talk a good fight, but when it comes down to the glass tacks, they're too lazy to produce.

I walked over to the stock tank and got myself a drink. Of course I was watching him out of the corner of my eye. He didn't notice, so I took another

drink, this one quite a bit louder than the first one. Nothing.

"Your tank's getting a little scum on the sides." Again, no response.

Well, it appeared that I had made my point— that I could go anywhere I pleased—and it appeared that he had given in and accepted my authority over the entire place. I was a little surprised that he had caved so soon. I mean, I hadn't even been forced to show fangs or bark or anything. I had expected more of a struggle.

Was I really so scary? Apparently so. Maybe my title had helped, Head of Ranch Security.

At that moment, Drover came over to the edge of the pen. He yawned and gave me his usual grin. "Oh, hi Hank. What are you doing in the horse pen?"

"Oh, just checking things out, establishing my presence, you might say. Come on in and get yourself a drink. The water's fine."

"Oh . . . I think I'll stay here. I'm kind of scared of horses."

"Why? Look at me." I pranced up and down, even stood up on my back legs and walked a few steps. Pretty daring, huh? You bet it was, but I had one eye on Billy the whole time, just in case.

But I needn't have worried about Billy. He'd

gotten so fat and lazy over the winter months, he wasn't going to bother anyone.

Drover was impressed. "Gosh, that's good. I figured the horse would get mad if a dog got in his pen."

"You just have to know how to handle horses, son. They're big and loud and overbearing at first, but if you're firm with 'em, they'll come around."

"I'll be derned. I bet you won't go sit on his hay."

I glanced at the three blocks of alfalfa on the ground, then turned back to Drover. "Why would you make such a foolish bet?"

"'Cause I don't think you'll do it. I wouldn't. You know how horses are about their feed."

I paused to think it over. I mean, I had made my point with Billy the Windbag Horse, and I didn't want to press my luck. On the other hand . . . hmm. I had been in his precious pen for ten whole minutes. I had taken a drink from his water tank, and I had even paraded around on my back legs. And he had done nothing about it, hadn't even said a word.

I had a feeling that I could pull it off. If he made a dive for me, I would scamper away and laugh at him. I was smaller and quicker, right? I had been blessed with remarkable speed and lightning-fast reflexes, right?

"All right, Drover, I'm going to do this for your benefit. It's part of your education. Watch and take notes."

You probably think I swaggered over and flopped down on the pile of hay. Nope. I was confident but not cocky. I moved toward the hay pile in stages: three steps, stop, wait, watch; three steps, stop, wait, watch. And the whole time I was doing this, I never once took my eyes off Billy. I mean, at the first sign of trouble, I was ready to hit the Afterburners and get myself out of range of his hooves.

That's what they do, you know. They try to kick you with their back feet or paw you with their front ones. As long as he had all four feet on the ground, I was in business.

I moved closer and closer. I was only three feet away from him, when all of a sudden . . .

CHAPTER TWELVE

Happy Ending or Good-bye to Slim?

Okay, relax. Billy swished his tail and the end of it brushed across my nose. It gave me a little scare, but I managed to keep control of things.

I inched forward, and by then I was only two feet from the hay pile. He was munching, flicking his ears now and then, and looking off to the north. If he was aware of my presence, he wasn't showing it. Well, that was all I needed to know. I took the last three steps and sat down in the middle of his alfalfa.

I beamed him a smile. "Hi."

His head swung around. He stopped chewing. Our eyes met, and he went right back to chewing. I tossed a glance toward Drover. "See? There's really nothing . . ."

HUH?

What a cheap trick. As you may know, when horses attack dogs, they're supposed to do it with their hooves, right? I mean, that's sort of the accepted method of operation amongst horses and dogs. We've been doing it that way for years, for centuries. Everybody knows the rules of the game and everybody . . .

But you know what he did? The instant, the very instant I took my eyes off of him, he reached down his head, clamped his big ugly green-stained teeth around the loose skin on my neck, picked me up, and flung me into the air. And we're talking about flying lessons, boys. I cleared the top of the fence and hit the ground like a rock.

OOF!

It knocked the wind out of me. Otherwise I might have gone charging back into the pen and thrashed the hateful thing. Or at least sprayed him with some stern barking. But I was doing well just to breathe. I staggered to my feet and tried to catch a breath.

Drover came rushing up. "Boy howdy, did you see that?"

I managed to gasp a reply. "Of course I saw it, you birdbrain. It was me!"

"Yeah, and boy, did you fly! I never saw a dog fly so far."

"Don't forget that he cheated. If he'd played by accepted rules, he never would have . . . help me to the porch, Drover, I'm badly wounded."

I dragged myself to the porch—to the sheet of plywood, I should say. There, I was able to regain the use of my breathing mechanisms. At that point I aimed a scorching glare back to the horse pen.

You know what Billy was doing? Nothing. Eating. Munching hay. He didn't gloat, he didn't laugh, he didn't even look at me. How do you suppose *that* made me feel? I mean, he had just thrown the Head of Security out of the corral, right? A major offense, an unspeakable crime. Yet to look at the oaf, you'd have thought he'd just swatted a fly.

I was outraged. "Okay, Drover, we've managed to gain valuable information from this experience, information that we can use against him in the future."

"Oh good. What is it?"

I leaned forward and whispered in his ear. "*He doesn't want dogs in his pen.*"

And so it was that our long and difficult search for Truth had ended in triumph.

I was about to enlighten Drover on the importance of Truth, but just then, Slim emerged from the chicken house. He came over to the porch and sat down. He reached out his hand and began scratching me behind the ears.

"Well, I'm done. Now it's time to move along, and I . . ." He left his thought hanging in the air. He hitched up his jeans and went inside the trailer. If he'd known I was listening, he probably wouldn't have sung his "Song of the Road," but he didn't notice me and I heard the whole thing. Here's how it went.

Song of the Road

Three pairs of socks in a grocery sack,
A couple of shirts and a well-used kack,
It doesn't take me long to gather up and pack,
And it's time to load 'em up and move along.

Ben Greene's books go along with me.
They tell of things I'd like to see.
A cowboy's life is wild and free,
And it's time to load 'em up and move along.

So good-bye, four walls,
I can hear the highway call,
It reminds me of the coyote's distant song.
It's been mostly lots of fun,
And now this deal nearly is done,

125

And it's time to load the truck and move
   along.

Sagebrush smells like a sweet perfume,
Snowflakes whisper a lonesome tune,
Memories here in this empty room,
And it's time to load 'em up and move along.

Two old shirts in a grocery sack
Remind me of all the things I lack.
I'm leaving soon and I'll not be back,
For it's time to load 'em up and move along.

So good-bye, four walls,
I can hear the highway call,
It reminds me of the coyote's distant song.
It's been mostly lots of fun,
And now this deal nearly is done,
And it's time to load the truck and move
   along.

When he finished the song, he looked up and
saw me. Our eyes met for a moment, and in that
moment a wave of great sadness washed over me.
Even though he had tried to throw me off course by
using words like "kack"—the old cowboy term for a
saddle—Slim's song made it pretty clear that he

wouldn't be going back to the ranch. I had tried not to think about it, but there it was. Slim was leaving us, and most likely, we would never see him again. All of our good times together had come to an end.

I saw the sadness in his eyes, but then he turned away and said in a gruff voice, "Don't you have anything better to do? Things change, pooch, and I've got to move on. I'll call Loper and tell him to come get y'all dogs."

Drover was there, and naturally he had to start moaning and groaning. "Gosh, Slim's not going back to the ranch?"

"That's what he said, Drover."

"And we'll go back without him?"

"That seems to be the plan, yes."

"Gosh, what'll we do on cold winter nights? Where will we sleep?"

"We'll sleep . . . I don't know where we'll sleep, but it'll probably be out in the cold somewhere."

His lip began to quiver. "I'm not sure I want to go back to the ranch if Slim's not going to be there."

I got up and marched a few steps away. "Drover, he's a cowboy. Cowboy's drift in and they drift out. A dog can't allow himself to get attached to them."

"Yeah, but I already have."

"Will you knock it off? This is going to be hard enough without you squalling and bawling about it."

"You're going to miss him too, aren't you?"

"No. Things change, Drover. People come and go. The only thing that stays the same is the ranch."

"Yeah, but the ranch won't be the same without Slim. Go ahead and admit it."

"No, I won't admit it."

Slim came, carrying two grocery sacks in his arms. They were stuffed with his worldly goods: shirts, socks, underpants, a pair of boots. He placed them on the seat on the passenger's side of his pickup, then went back inside for one last look around. He heaved a sigh, closed the door, and walked to the pickup, with his head down and a grim expression on his face.

He pointed to the back of the pickup and said, "Load up, dogs, one last time." He fired up the pickup and we resumed our journey, all of us covered with a heavy blanket of sadness.

Since Slim's pickup was illegal to drive, and since he didn't want to move into the "Crossbar Hotel" (his term for jail), he took the back roads and side streets into town.

He was pretty sly about it. Before he pulled out into a street, he stopped and looked in all directions for the police car. Only then did he creep out into the street and resume the journey to Leonard's Saddle Shop.

We had gotten to within a block of Leonard's place when . . . imagine Slim's surprise when we drove past an alley, and there sat the holstein-colored car that belonged to the city police. Slim saw the car but pretended he didn't. He drove on, holding his breath.

The police car didn't move. We crept on down the street. It appeared that we had dodged a bullet when . . . thirty-seven flashing lights came on and the police car shot out of the alley. Slim let out a groan and pulled over.

The policeman got out and walked up to the window. "Morning. You're Slim Chance, aren't you?"

"Yes sir, and I know . . ."

"Follow me to the courthouse, please."

"Yes sir."

We followed the patrol car through town. Drover had held up pretty well, but now he fell apart.

"Oh my gosh, they're going to throw Slim in jail, and what'll become of us?"

"I don't know, Drover. If we're lucky, maybe they'll let us go with him."

"Yeah, but what if we're not so lucky? Do you reckon they'll send us to the dog pound?"

I swallowed a big lump in my throat. "I guess we'll find out."

At last our sad little column reached the county

courthouse. Slim eased the pickup into a parking space, shut off the motor, heaved a deep sigh, and started to get out. He glanced to his left and saw . . . a cowboy leaning against the side of a pickup. His face was hidden beneath the brim of his hat. Slim narrowed his eyes.

I studied him too—the stranger, that is. Wasn't there something familiar about him? His scuffed boots, the tongue of his belt sticking out, the crease of his . . . HUH? Surely that wasn't . . .

Slim's brows shot up and his mouth dropped open. "Loper? Is that you?"

The stranger raised his head. It *was* Loper. "Just where the heck have you been?"

"Well, I've . . . I've been shoveling chicken manure, if you must know."

Loper nodded. "That was probably a smart career move. You never had much talent for cow-boying."

"By grabs, it's honest work, and I ain't a burden to the man who hired me."

Loper shook his head and walked over to Slim's window. "Look, I'm sorry I loaded you down with my problems. I should have kept my mouth shut."

"No, you should have done what you did. You told me the truth."

"I told you what was worrying me. The truth is

that I met with the banker yesterday afternoon and everything went fine."

"You mean . . ."

"I mean we're in business for another year, and the cattle market's headed up."

"I'll be derned. You mean . . ."

"Your job's waiting for you—if you can tear yourself away from the chicken house business."

"Huh. That'll be easy. But Loper, I think they're fixing to throw me in jail." He jerked his head toward the officer, who was standing nearby with his arms crossed.

"Well, a couple of months in jail might do you some good. But lucky for you," Loper smiled, "I've already worked this out with the authorities." He pointed toward the policeman and handed Slim a new license plate. "Put this on, get this rattletrap inspected, and head for the ranch. We've got two weeks' work to do before sundown."

Slim stared at him. "Well, it sounds just like the good old days. Thanks, Loper. Much as I want to see Alpine, I sure wasn't ready to leave the ranch."

So there you are. Slim didn't have to leave us after all and everything turned out for the best. You'll be glad to know that by four o'clock that afternoon, I was back in my position as Head of Ranch Security, making my rounds, barking at monsters, and preparing to take the ranch through another dangerous night.

That's a pretty good place to shut down this story, don't you think?

Case closed.

What's in store for the Head of Ranch Security?

In his next adventure, Hank the Cowdog must defend his ranch from coyotes, a saddle thief, and countless other monstrous critters. Of course, it's all in a day's work for the fearless Head of Ranch Security. Turn the page for a look at what Hank's up against in *Hank the Cowdog #35: The Case of the Saddle House Robbery.*

Code Three

My ears began picking up an odd sound. My left ear shot up, twisted around, and homed in on the sound. Holy smokes, *we had an unidentified vehicle approaching the ranch!*

I leapt up and began barking the alarm. "Drover, we've got a Code Three coming into headquarters! Get into Bark-the-Car Formation and let's check it out."

"Gosh, is it serious?"

"Every unauthorized penetration of the ranch is serious, Drover, and some are even more serious than others. Get into formation and let's move out."

He did, and we went swooping around the south side of the house. Boy, you should have seen us! Twenty-five yards out, we began a withering barrage of barking. Seconds later, we had the vehicle surrounded and had forced it to stop in front of the house.

Pretty impressive, huh? You bet it was, but that was just the beginning. Once we had this guy pulled over and stopped, I sprang into action and began shouting orders.

"Okay, Drover, prepare to Mark Tires! You take the right side. I've got the left side."

"Should we give 'em a Full Mark or a Short Squirt?"

"Short Squirt. We haven't run a check on these people and we don't know their intentions. It could be dangerous, so, yes, dart in there and do a Short Squirt. We can always go back later and do a better job. Move out!"

You should have seen us in action. It was poetry in motion. All our skill as dogs, all our training, all our dedication to duty came out in this exercise. Drover swooped in and knocked out both tires on the right side, and I've got to give the little mutt credit. He held his fire, took careful aim, and placed the ordinance in the target area.

Sometimes he doesn't do it that well, you know. I've seen times when he's lost control and started firing wild shots in all directions, but this time he delivered the goods.

2

Me? Well, I stepped up to the left front tire and *blasted* it. Hey, when you hit a tire with such force and accuracy that it makes the hubcap ring, you know you've done the job right. And that's just what I did, made that rascal ring like a bell.

I was tempted to linger and give it another round, but I had called for the Short Squirt Procedure, and timing is very important in this maneuver. If I had lingered even two or three seconds, it would have thrown off all our timing, which might have . . . I don't know what might have happened, but it could have had serious consequences. My buddy was working the other side, following a very precise timing schedule, and I had to do the same.

Teamwork, see. We're part of a team, an elite team of highly trained dogs who . . . all at once this seems kind of boring. Let's move on.

Okay, I lobbed a blast into Tire #1 and ran at full speed to Tire #2. The second tire is always the tougher in a Two-Tire Situation. For one thing, a guy has to reload on the run. For another thing, you've got the problem of exhaustion and dehydration. And finally, by the time we get to the second tire, we sometimes draw enemy fire.

See, the left side of the vehicle is more dangerous than the right, because the steering wheel and so forth are on the left side, and that's where the driver sits. Are you getting the picture? When we draw fire, it usually comes from the driver.

I know this is pretty technical stuff, and you probably had no idea that marking tires could be so complicated. Well, it is. Anything worth doing is worth being complicated. We don't just blunder in there and start squirting tires. Some mutts do, but Drover and I are the elite forces of the Security Division, and we figure that anything worth doing . . . I've already said that.

I had just fought my way to Tire #2, when suddenly and all of a sudden, the door flew open and an angry man leaped out. See, some drivers resent dogs marking their tires. It makes 'em mad and sometimes they yell and screech and try to disrupt our mission. We have a response to this. We call it "Too Bad." We go right on with the mission and ignore their threats and noise.

No ordinary dog would dare to do that, but here at the ranch, we do it all the time.

Okay, this guy leaped out of the pickup and . . . hang on, this gets a little scary . . . and he didn't respond with the usual stuff—you know, the yelling and hissing and so forth. No sir. He did things I'd never seen before, things to which we hadn't been trained to respond. To. To respond to. Two "to"s.

Are you ready for this?

I'm not so sure you are. It's so shocking, you may want to think about it for a minute.

If you decide to skip over the scary part, that'll be okay. We'll regroup on the other side, see, and nobody will call you a . . . well, a weenie, for example, or any other tacky name. No name-calling here. Honest.

You be the judge.

Okay, I guess some of you are still with me. Thanks. This'll be pretty rough, and I'm glad to have your support in troubled times.

Here we go. This guy didn't just step out and yell. He LEAPED out, made claws with his hands, made fangs with his teeth, and came RUNNING toward me! Oh, and he was also GROWLING! And he had a horrible ugly face. Horrible.

Honest. This is no exaggeration.

What kind of person would do such things? I had no idea. The man was obviously some kind of . . . I don't know what. A disturbed person, perhaps even . . .

We fed all our information straight into Data Control, and got back a shocking message. It said that this guy had all the markings and so-forths of . . . you'd better hang on for this . . . a *vampire!*

Don't laugh. Vampires growl and bite and

show their teeth, right? And they're ugly, right?

When an unauthorized vehicle pulls up in front of the house, we never know who or what it might contain. Maybe it's a family out for a Sunday drive in the country, but maybe it's not. Maybe it's a carload of . . . vampires or grave-robbers or escaped crinimals or . . . we never know.

We try not to think about such things. I mean, we have a job to do and we can't dwell on all the terrible things that could happen to us when we're performing a Short Squirt Procedure.

And there I was. I had just moved into position and was about to initiate the procedure on the rear tire, when this lunatic vampire came flying out the door, made claws, made teeth, started growling, and came lurching toward me.

I was frozen by fear. Never in my entire career had I seen anything quite like this. I saw the veins bulging in his horrible eyes. I even saw . . . or thought I saw . . . *blood* dripping off his fangs. In a flash, I threw all circuits over to Data Control's Master Program, and things started happening real fast. Right away, we got a warning light on the Coolant Panel. The cryogenic cooling system that ran the Squirt Program had just failed. We were getting nothing but tiny droplets through the system. All at once, the mission was on hold.

Then, seconds later, we got a second alarm, this one even more frightening than the first. Master Control had gone to Condition Red, and we had gotten the order to go to *Vampire Counter-measures.*

Perhaps you're surprised that we had trained for this contagency. We had. Even though the chances of finding vampires on the ranch were pretty low, we had prepared for it. Our training called for a rapid, multilayered response. Would you like to take a peek at it? I don't suppose it would hurt.

First thing, we went to Full Flaps on the ears— jumped 'em up to their very highest position. Next, we uttered a code word that locked in the Vamp-Count program. The code word, in case you'd like to know, was . . . "HUH?" That short, three-letter word kicked in Vampire Countermeasures, and things started happening real fast.

We went to Full Reverse on all engines and began moving backward at a high rate of speed, but at the same time, we launched a bark that was intended to freeze the emeny in his tracks. The enemy, I should say, freeze the enemy in his tracks.

Well, it didn't work. He kept coming, slouching, growling, and making threatening gestures with his teeth, eyes, and claws. We launched a second bark, this one even bigger than the first. We had to do something to stop the guy, or at least slow his rate of attack.

He kept coming.

Well, by this time it had become crystal clear that this was no ordinary vampire. *He ate dogs.* And fellers, once our intelligence network had established this fact, we had pretty muchly run out of options. We had trained for Moderate Vampires, not Serious Vampires, and all at once our hands were cut out for us.

Up in the cockpit, I heard the voice of Master Control: "Uh, Lone Ranger, we're showing a Condition Dark Red. We need to get you out of there right away. We're switching you over to the Sell-the-Farm Program. Take cover, and good luck, soldier."

There you are. You heard it from the voice of Master Control, just as I did, and no doubt you shared with me the tension and seriousness of the moment. Pretty scary, huh? You bet it was, but I tried to warn you.

Are you still with me? Hang on. We're not out of the woods yet.

Okay, let's back up for a second. Master Control broke in on our normal communications channel and told us to switch to the Sell-the-Farm Program, right? This was a deeply coded message and you're probably wondering what it meant. That's the whole purpose of codes, see, to confuse the enemy.

Maybe you knew that.

In our code system (we were using the Ultra Confuso code that month) we didn't use such battle terms as run, Mayday, retreat, or help. Those were common words, and they were known to our enemies, so we had a heavily coded expression that meant the same thing: *Sell-the-Farm*.

Pretty clever, huh? Good thing I'm here to explain all this stuff.

Well, when my inner ears picked up that coded message, I prepared to eject and scuttle the ship— or, to keep within the perambulates of the coding system, to "Sell the Farm." Things happened very fast. I abandoned the Marking Procedure and blew out of there in a cloud of dust, leaving the savage vampire to wonder how I had managed to escape the clutches of his clutch.

Here's how I did it. You'll be impressed, I think. See, instead of running far away, as most ordinary dogs would have done, I *pretended* to run far away and wiggled myself beneath the vampire's pickup—the very last place a vampire would look for his victim.

Awesome, huh?

And once hidden in the basement of his pickup, I assumed the Stealthy Crouch Position, which means that I neither moved nor breathed nor nothinged, and therefore became invisible to Vampire Vision and even enemy radar.

There . . . I waited. The silence, the tension, the pressure were almost unbearable. My ears picked up the sound of footsteps, yet I remained in the Frozen Stealth Position. I dared not move. Then, out of the corner of my periphery, I saw . . .

HUH?

Have you read all of Hank's adventures?

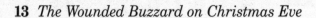